THE TUNNEL

THE TUNNEL

JAMES F. CAUSEY

LAGRANGE GEORGIA

iSeebookz Publishing
Suite 137B Commerce Ave #300
Lagrange GA 30241

Cover cosmic illustrated art by Lee Cook
Editor Y. D. Rowland

ISBN 979-8-985-4863-4-6

First Edition
10 9 8 7 6 5 4 3 2 1

This is a work of fiction. To preserve the authenticity of the author's voice and essence of thought, minimal editing has been performed in segments. We extend our appreciation for your support.

iSeebookz Publishing/ James Causey

DEDICATION

My sincere appreciation goes to all who helped in this journey. This book is dedicated to my daughter Kayla and my grandchildren and all my readers and supporters. Because of you, I am inspired to write more.

Thank you.

James

Contents

PROLOGUE

It was seven days before Tom West's sixteenth birthday when his mother and father were killed in an automobile accident. Unfortunately, due to the lack of guardianship, the sheriff of Chilton County placed him in a foster home.

However, Tom had other plans, and within two days, he ran away and returned to his home in Verbena, Alabama. Walter Cannon, his wife Faye, and their daughter Holly lived down the road from Tom. Noticing a need, Walter told the sheriff he would look out for the boy.

It wasn't long before Holly and Tom became the best of friends, and their life adventure became a written book- for no one would ever believe them if it was told as the truth...

1

The Gold Box

Two years later

Tom sat on the bank of Chestnut Creek, his cane pole stretched out over the water, and the red-white bobber floated gently downstream. His mind was on Holly. It was her birthday, and he wanted to do something she wouldn't have expected.

He picked up his stringer of fish and started up the path. Then, as he held the fish before him, a thought came. He made a decision. *They would make a fine meal. I am going to cook her dinner,* he thought as he looked out into the sky. It had been a good day for fishing, and looking at what he had caught, he felt proud of himself.

The noon sun glared upon the earth until it bounced off an object. A beam of reflected light caught Tom's attention as an object sat directly in his path. He placed his hand above his eyes to block the glare. It had been a few hours since he walked down the path to go fishing, and the object hadn't been there earlier. Tom turned around and looked for its owner, as he thought someone must have placed it on the path or left it by mistake. Not seeing anyone, Tom called out. "Hello. Is anyone there?"

When no one answered, he walked up to the shiny object, laid his fish and cane pole onto the ground, and reached down and picked it up. He shook his head from side to side in disbelief; the object was a box made of gold. He ran straight to his truck, and in his excitement, he forgot his cane pole and fish. He laughed at himself, placed the gold box on the seat of his truck, and then walked back down the path to retrieve his forgotten items.

Tom returned to his truck, still puzzled over who had left the box. He looked around again, seeing no one; he shrugged his shoulders, opened the door, got in his truck, and set out for the two-mile journey to reach his home. Tom carried the box inside, sat it on the kitchen table, and put the fish on ice. He glanced off and on as he paced in front of his table, scratching the back of his head before massaging his neck as he thought, then he pulled out a chair and sat down.

He picked up the box and shook it. Nothing rattled from the inside. He turned the box over, studying all sides, and noticed some strange writing on the front of it, but Tom couldn't remember seeing anything like it. There was also a tiny hole on the box's front side. *This could be for a key*, he thought. Hearing the clock ticking on the wall, Tom realized the time. He got up and placed the box on a shelf inside one of the kitchen cabinets. Tom knew he would have to figure it out later. He still needed to drive to Marbury, pick up Holly's cake, then clean and cook the fish.

~~~~

Holly Cannon lay across her bed as she thought about the day's events. It was her twentieth birthday. Once again, her mother and father had gone all out for her and like all other birthdays, their day started with a trip to the Birmingham Zoo, which was okay with her. She loved the zoo and hoped this would be one place she would never outgrow. Her presents were mostly clothes, which was alright with her. Holly thought about starting college in the fall, and she needed all the clothes she could get.

Her mind returned to the purple envelope and its contents, consisting of a beautiful card and a small gold key. The envelope and the card had yet to be signed. Holly put the key on a chain and placed it around her neck. She believed that whoever gave the key would say something, and she would know who had given it to her.

She looked at the clock on her nightstand. It was seven fifteen p.m. She had promised her friend Tom she would be at his house around eight, so she needed to get going. It was a twenty-minute walk, and it would be dark soon. She didn't know why, but she had been afraid of the dark ever since she was a little girl.

Holly ran down the stairs and told her mother she was going to visit Tom and would be home around ten. Not giving her mother time to respond, she ran out the door. Once outside, she slowed to a fast walk. The sun was almost behind the trees, and their shadows covered the road. Once
~~~~

again, she ran. Tom's house sat fifty yards off the road; by the time she reached his steps, it was dark. She stopped long enough to catch her breath. She didn't want Tom to know she had been running. He would make fun of her fears, and she hated when he did this.

When he heard the screen door slam, Tom knew Holly had arrived. "Happy Birthday!" he yelled as she walked into the kitchen. He had cleaned and cooked the fish, along with French fries and hush puppies. The table had been set with a small cake as its centerpiece. He wanted to surprise her, and the smile on her face told him he had done a great job.

After they had finished eating, Holly stood, walked around the table, put her arms around Tom, and kissed him on the cheek. "Thank you, but you know you didn't have to do all of this," she said, waving her arm across the table. "I know, but you know how I feel about you," he said. Then, before Holly could respond. Tom held up his hand. "I understand. We have already talked about this, college first, which reminds me that I may have found a way to pay my way through college."

Holly tilted her head as Tom walked over to the cabinet, picked up the gold box, and placed it on the table before her. "Where did you get this?" She asked.

"I found it on the ground down by the creek." Holly stared at the box silently for a few minutes, and then a memory came to mind.

"I've seen this writing somewhere." She turned and looked at Tom. "Hey, do you remember that old painting inside our barn? It has several scenes. There is a mountain covered in snow, an old house, a river, and I swear this same writing is at the bottom of it." Tom thought about what Holly had described, and his memories came flooding back.

"Yes, I saw it but never really paid much attention to it. What do you think those words mean?" Tom asked. Holly shrugged her shoulders as she picked up the box to examine it. She noticed the small hole and sat the box back down. Remembering the item around her neck. "Hey Tom, check this out." She said as she took the small gold key from around her neck and gave it to Tom. He looked at the key, then at the small hole.

"What do you think?" Holly asked.

"Something doesn't seem right about this," Tom said as he pushed the key inside the hole.

~~~~

Walter Cannon walked into the kitchen as Faye stared out the window. "How did it go?" she asked without turning around. "I believe it went well. I followed our plan. I placed the box on the path between Tom's truck, but then I had to hide again because he left his fish and cane pole. He came back for them." Walter said with a little smile, thinking about Tom's reaction.

"Do you think they will come back?" Faye asked.
"Of course, we came back," Walter stated with conviction.

"I know, but we knew ahead of time what to expect. I wish we could have told them."

Walter walked over and put his arms around Faye. "Look, those kids are smart. They will figure this out and be back before you know it." Faye turned around with tears running down her face. "I guess you're right, and I did leave the letter, plus the old man said he would take care of them."
~~~~

Walter patted her back as he comforted her. "Go get some sleep. You will feel better about this in the morning."

As Faye left the room, Walter opened the refrigerator and took out a beer. When he closed the fridge, he saw the picture of Holly on her sixteenth birthday that Faye had pinned on the door with a magnet. In the picture, Holly stood beside her new bike. She had no interest in driving, so he had brought her a ten-speed. The bike had small tires, and they didn't last long, with them living along the dirt road. The bike ended up inside the barn, alongside all the other toys Holly had outgrown.

Walter took the picture from the fridge, carried it to his man cave, and sat on the couch. Laying his head back on the sofa after swallowing a big gulp of beer. He let his mind wander to when he believed it all started.

2

Pay the Price

Walter met Faye while they were in high school. The two of them sat next to one another in most of their classes. It wasn't until Faye asked him to the Valentine's Day dance that they started dating. After high school, he enrolled at U.C.L.A. Walter wanted to be a doctor and had been told this was the best college for receiving his Ph.D. Faye had enrolled in the nursing school at U.A.B. college in Birmingham, but one week before he was to leave for California, she informed him she would be going with him.

After arriving in California, they decided to rent a small apartment off-campus so they could stay together. Doing this meant he had to take a part-time job. He worked three times a week from eight p.m. until two a.m. at a convenience store. Not many people came in after midnight, thus giving him time to study.

One night, around eleven, two men walked into the

store. He laid his books down and stood as they approached the counter. One of them pulled a gun from his jacket and pointed it at him. The man demanded the money. He had been told if anything like this happened, he was to do whatever they asked. He took all the money out of the drawer and put it on the counter, which totaled forty-three dollars and some change. This caused the man to get angry. It was then he shot him in the face.

At that point, all Walter could remember was the bright light. He couldn't tell where the light came from. He couldn't hear or speak, but he knew he wasn't dead because he had the ability to think. As the light faded, Walter noticed someone standing next to him. An old man reached out and took his hand, and at that moment, it was as if he was a bystander outside his body, looking down at himself. His head had been bandaged, and he had tubes up his nose and down his throat. Faye was kneeling beside the bed with her head bowed as if she was praying. The old man began to speak, and Walter turned to face him.

"Find a man who goes by the name W. L. Benson," was all he said. Then he disappeared, and darkness came. He didn't know how long he had been unconscious. He tried to speak, but no words came out. When he tried to open his eyes, only one of them opened. Faye sat in a chair beside the bed, holding his hand. When he was able to squeeze her hand, she stood. He saw the tears that had stained her cheeks.

The next day, the doctor and nursing staff came in and removed the tubes. Walter looked and watched, curious about his overall condition. But all he could do was wait. After attending to his immediate needs and clearing him of the medical equipment that had assisted him while he was unconscious, the doctor began to speak.

"You have been through an awful ordeal. We were hoping for the best, and it was all down to you waking up." Faye nodded as tears ran down her face to the side of a wide grin of gratitude that he had awakened.

Walter took it all in with his ears. Still curious and hoping the doctor would quickly explain what was happening and what might happen next with his health. The doctor told him straight and to the point.

Telling Walter he had been shot and had to remove part of his skull, which left a dent on the side of his head. The doctor continued...explaining that he was blind in the right eye and it may be possible he would regain his speech.

Faye stayed by his side for three weeks after the shooting before returning to school. His mother and father flew from Alabama; they stayed in his and Faye's rental apartment. Two months later, he was released from the hospital and flew back to Alabama with his parents.

Six Years Later

Six years had passed before Faye returned to Alabama. Walter sat on the front porch of his father's house, waiting for Faye. He also held onto a note he had written to himself several times over the years. The older man's words had haunted him. He believed the time had come to do what the man had asked. He stood when he saw Faye's car pull into the drive. He saw her smile as she got out of the car. She walked up the steps and kissed him. He handed her the note.

"What is this?" She asked as she unfolded the piece of paper. After she read the note, she looked at him curiously and asked, "Why haven't you told me about this before now?" Although his words were slurred, Faye understood when he said he didn't think she would believe him. It was then that Faye told Walter to get in her car. She explained that W.L. Benson was her grandfather, and she was taking him to Georgia, where her grandfather lived. Walter was dumbfounded by how long he had lived, haunted by the message all because of doubt as he looked at Faye while they drove to Georgia.

Three hours later, Faye parked her car in front of W.L. Benson's house. He met them at the door. Seeing his granddaughter and looking at her guest, W.L. said nothing but gave an upward hmph for a greeting. Faye and Walter followed as he held the door open for them to enter his home. Walking past them after they crossed his threshold, W.L. led them to the back of his house, where they went to a small room with a small table and two chairs. A gold box sat on the table. W.L. extended his arm, motioning for Walter and Faye to enter the room and sit in the chairs.

They looked at the box and then around the nondecorated room. The gold box seemed out of place and glittered in the dim light. Taking out a pipe and commencing to light it, W.L. Benson leaned against the door frame as he puffed and blew out smoke. Looking at the box, he pointed his pipe to it. He began giving instructions as he commanded their complete attention, with a look dead into each of their eyes as if to say. *Do as I tell you!*

Walter considered leaving, but W.L. Benson's stance at the door stated otherwise. "You two will go down a mountain, then follow a river downstream until you come across a cabin."

Walter looked at him, not understanding what he was saying until the following statement.

'There is an old man who lives there,' he said as he looked at Walter and his granddaughter. He can help your friend here, Walter, right?" W.L. Benson said as he turned again to Walter. Walter nodded. W.L. Benson handed Faye a small gold key and gave a simple command: "Use it."

Faye held the key and then looked at the box. Noticing the small hole in the front of it, she inserted the key and asked Walter if he was ready. Walter looked at her questioningly. *Ready for what?* He didn't know, but he nodded as Faye turned the key.

~~~~

A bright light hit Walter in his face. He couldn't see Faye but felt her presence. When the light faded, he stood looking down a mountain with snow covering his shoes. He could see out of both eyes; then he spoke her name.

Faye ran to him smiling, threw her arms around his neck, and kissed him. Walter glanced at Faye. She looked different. He looked at his hands and was amazed at all that had occurred. If he could see and talk. It should not be alarming that they both felt and looked seven years younger.

Following W.L. Benson's instructions, they started walking. A little way down the mountain, they came upon a cave. The glow from the inner fire drew them.
~~~~

Once inside the cave, they saw that someone had built a fire, prepared some food, and laid out two sleeping bags. Trusting W.L., they settled in for the night, speaking briefly of Walter's recovery and the wonder of their youth. They slept until morning.

Upon waking, they readied themselves and continued to travel down the mountain. It was nearing nightfall when they found another fire and more food. Again, they slept until morning before continuing their journey.

Another day had passed before they reached the river. Faye wanted to follow the river at night, but Walter decided it would be best to wait until morning.

The following day, Walter was awakened by the morning sun shining on his face. Faye was still sleeping, so he decided to take a walk along the river. It seemed like they had walked from winter into spring. The mountain was cold, the snow deep, but along the river, there was green grass with trees full of leaves, and he could hear the birds singing. He looked at his reflection in the river. He was Walter again. There was no dent on the side of his head, and his right eye was back in place. He picked up a small stone and dropped it into the water, causing his reflection to ripple.

At that time, he asked himself the question, "Is this really happening, or will I soon awake from a dream?"

~~~~

Walter and Faye spent most of the day walking along the river before they found the cabin. Walking up to the door, curious as to what's next since they arrived at their destination, Walter opened the door and stepped inside without knocking. Faye followed behind him. The room was small,
~~~~

decorated with a table and four chairs. A young boy sat in one of the chairs. A gold box rested on the table in front of him. "Close the door." The young boy said.

Walter and Faye turned and looked at the already closed door. When they looked back, the young boy had turned into an old man. "Have a seat," he said.

Although it had been seven years since he heard the sound of his voice, Walter knew this was the old man who told him to find W.L. Benson. Walter and Faye sat across from the old man.

"Why the young boy?" Walter asked curiously, full of questions he felt the older man could answer.

Chuckling before he spoke, "That was a ploy to show you this is a world of change."

"Why the long journey from the mountain to the river and from the river to here?" Walter asked.

The old man, now amused, laughed and stated, "It's my way of testing your dedication to the cause."

"And what cause would that be?" Walter asked.

The old man stood. A mirror appeared in his hand, which he handed to Walter. "Look at yourself, then remember what you looked like before you came here. You are the cause, Walter," he said.

The older man reached inside his pocket and brought out a small gold key. He held it up in front of them.

"The box on the table will send you back to your world. You will arrive on the night you were shot. The men who shot you will not appear. The two of you may continue your lives as planned, but for this, there will be a price to pay. The two of you will marry. You will have a daughter. There will also be a boy. You will raise him as your own. On your daughter's twentieth birthday, you will send her and the boy to me. I will give them a task and send them back to you once it is completed. There is one important factor here that you must remember. Walter and Faye looked at each other, questioning. *How much more of their future lives would he tell?* Looking at them both after regaining their attention, he spoke calmly yet sternly.

"In no way, form, or fashion are you to tell them about this world." The old man pointed his finger toward the table. A pen and a simple sheet of paper appeared. "You may take your time to write a letter giving them instructions on how to find me. I personally will leave the letter inside the cave."

Faye, pleased with the future but worried about her future children, asked a valid question.

"How will we send them if we cannot tell them where they are going?"

Again, the older man laughed. "It will be simple. You will give one the key and the other the golden box. Curiosity will send them here," he said.

~~~~

Walter set the beer bottle on the coffee table. The old man had been true to his word. He and Faye had lived a life most people dream of, but now it was time to pay the price.
~~~~

3

The Tunnel

Tom turned the key, and the room spun around him. Blinded by the bright light, he closed his eyes and yelled for Holly, but she didn't answer. The spinning continued as he felt himself falling, and with a soft impact, he landed on something cold and wet. When he opened his eyes, his face was buried in snow. He raised his head and saw that Holly lay beside him. Reaching over and grabbing her arm, Tom pulled her to him. She opened her eyes. "Are you okay?" he asked.

Holly shook the snow from her face. "What the hell happened?" she yelled. Tom didn't answer right away. He was just as baffled as she was. He stood and noticed there was a cave behind them. Turning away from the cave, he looked down the mountain and then to Holly.

"Now, this may sound crazy, but I believe we are inside that painting." Holly looked at him skeptically. "You are crazy. You and I both know that isn't possible."

Tom took Holly by her shoulders and turned around in a circle. "Look, we are standing on a mountain covered with snow. There is a cave behind us, and you can see the river when you look down the mountain," Tom stated as Holly laughed.

"This isn't funny, Holly. It's serious."

Holly, not wanting to believe what was right in front of her, tried to reason logic into Tom's crazy idea. "Think, Tom, there are only two logical explanations for this. Either we are both dreaming the same dream, or we are both dead." Tom reached over and pinched Holly on her arm.

"Ouch, Why did you do that for?" Rubbing her arm to dull the pain inflicted. Tom laughed as he proved his point. "We are not dead."

Holly began to realize there may be some truth to his answer, but she remained skeptical. "What are we going to do now?"

Tom looked around and then pointed in a direction. "Let's go check out that cave. It's cold out here, and we need shelter." Holly agreed as the wind picked up and blew a colder breeze, making her realize her clothes were not made for the weather.

Walking inside the cave, it took a few minutes for their eyes to adjust to the darkness. They saw a large trunk, and the lid had been left open. On top of what looked like blankets lay a box of matches and a folded sheet of paper. Tom struck one of the matches when he noticed a circle of rocks and a stalk of wood on the cave floor. Within minutes, he had a fire going. Holly unfolded the sheet of paper and sat by the fire to read it aloud.

To our daughter,

I pray you and the boy are safe. I know it's hard for you and the boy to understand what has happened. We promise we will explain everything once you are back home. But for now, be brave. You must travel down the mountain until you arrive at the river. Follow it downstream until you see a cabin. The old man who lives there will help you return (home). We want you to know we love you.

Mom & Dad.

Holly looked up from her reading. "Tom, this letter doesn't tell us where we are, how we got here, nor why we are even here." Tom stirred the fire to get more fire to burn before he walked over to the cave entrance to look outside. Turning around to answer her question, he saw a log on the outskirts of a flame. Reaching for another piece of kindle, he repositioned the firewood before he spoke.

"Holly, those are more questions than answers; we can do nothing about it right now. Plus, it is getting dark, so we can stay here tonight. Tomorrow, we will go down this mountain and find that old man. Even if that letter wasn't written for us, maybe he can provide some answers."

~~~~

The next morning, Holly held on to Tom as they made their way down a narrow path. At the end of the day, Tom estimated they had traveled six or eight miles. From where he stood looking down at the river, they had at least another five miles to go. He saw a small section of flat ground
~~~~

between two large boulders. They decided to camp there for the night. Tom managed to find enough dry wood to build a fire. The two of them huddled together, wishing they had brought the blankets. However, It wasn't long before they drifted off to sleep.

The sun had risen above the trees, and when Tom woke up, Holly was nowhere in sight. He yelled her name several times, and his panic increased when she didn't answer. Tom continued to walk down the narrow path, calling Holly's name every few minutes. As he approached a curve in the path, he heard people laughing. Tom, questioning himself, began to run down the path and felt relief when he saw Holly, then fear because she wasn't alone. He couldn't believe his eyes. Holly was talking to a man who wore a long red robe, and he had a gold crown atop his head.

When Tom got closer, he noticed a woman was also among them. By appearance, she looked no older than he and Holly. She wore a pair of faded jeans, a sweatshirt, and a pair of Nike running shoes. As soon as Holly saw Tom, she ran to meet him. "Who are those people?" he asked. Holly grabbed his hand, pulling him toward them. "The man is a king, and he owns a castle on the other side of the mountain. But the best part is he knows the old man and will help us find him." Tom listened closely as Holly expressed the next statement almost breathlessly. "He said we don't need the old man because he can help us go home. Can you believe our luck… we can be sent back home through what he calls "The Tunnel".

Tom looked into Holly's eyes, hearing all she had said and remembering the letter from the cave; he looked at her with doubtful eyes. "Holly, do you think we can trust him?"

Holly did not like that Tom was not delighted with the information presented. However, she was still not convinced about all that had taken place. "Listen, Tom, I'm unsure if any of this is real, including that letter. It's not a matter of trust. It's about being smart. We go along with them for now, and if anything seems wrong, we have to be ready to bail." Tom considered all that Holly had said as he introduced himself to the so-called King. Tom stood before the man, thinking about bowing, but instead, he stuck out his hand.

"Hi, I'm Tom West. It is a pleasure to meet you, sir." The man reached out and shook Tom's hand. "Hello, my name is King Dusten, and this young lady is my loyal friend Stella. It is my honor to meet the both of you," he said.

Tom nodded and decided to follow Holly's lead. They went down the mountain with the King and Stella. Turning north on another path, they came to an open road. Tom and Holly stopped in their tracks. Nothing should have surprised them at that point, but the sight of the king's carriage and the six beautiful white horses took their breath away, along with the two men dressed in black, from head to toe, standing beside the carriage.

One of the men held the door open. The other man climbed atop the carriage and picked up the reins. The King climbed in first. Stella stood aside, allowing Tom and Holly to enter before her. Once inside, the man closed the door and climbed atop the carriage. It moved slowly at first, then picked up speed as they traveled down a winding dirt road. Tom felt Holly's head touch his shoulder. Holly, the King, and Stella fell asleep, and Tom looked out the window to pass the time. The carriage made it down the mountain and was traveling on flat ground.

Observing the scenery, Tom swore they could have been back in Alabama. The carriage passed by two cotton fields only to travel alongside a pasture sometime later. Tom saw cows, horses, goats, and even thought he saw a few deer mixed in with them. He wanted Holly to see but decided not to wake her. Instead, he rested his head on the soft seat and closed his eyes. When he opened them, Holly, Stella, and the King were all looking at him. "What?" he asked curiously, slightly annoyed by their questioning look.

It was the King who spoke. "We are a few minutes from the castle. Now you have a choice. You may enter the castle walls, or you may continue your journey in search of the old man. If you choose to enter, I will show how and why you have come to this world."

"Will you help us return home?" Holly asked before Tom could speak.

"Yes, but first, there is something you must do for me." The King replied.

"And what would that be?" Tom asked.

"I'll explain that later, but I need your decision right now."

Tom looked at Holly, and she nodded her head. Tom, looking at Holly and seeing her relaxing, stated. "We will go inside."

The carriage moved slowly alongside the castle walls. Tom could see guards posted on top of the walls, which he thought was funny. For some strange reason, he expected the guards to be dressed in some sixteenth-century outfit. Instead, the guards were dressed in camouflage, each carrying what looked like Army-issued M.16 assault rifles. The King saw the confusion on Tom's face.

"Are you having second thoughts?" he asked.

"Oh, no, sir. It's just. .. well, Sir, once you explain why we are here, I will feel better about our situation."

"I'm sure you will," the King said.

There was a moat around the castle. A bridge had been lowered, and the large wooden gates were swung open. The sound of the horses crossing the bridge sent chills down Tom's spine. He reached over and took Holly's hand, looking into her eyes, seeing her now concerned. "We are going to be Okay, Holly," he said to reassure her.

The carriage came to a stop in front of two large doors. The King exited the carriage first. By the time Tom, Holly, and Stella had climbed out, the king had disappeared inside the castle.

"Follow Me," Stella said.

Tom realized those were the first words he had heard Stella speak. "Where are we going?" he asked.

"There is always a meal prepared in one of the dining halls. I don't know about the two of you, but I'm starved."

Once again, Tom and Holly couldn't believe their eyes. Although there were only four chairs, the table was at least forty feet long, with food stacked from one end to the other. The plates, cups, and forks were all made of gold. Stella immediately sat in a chair and started eating, then looked at Tom and Holly.

"What are you waiting for? Eat, Eat."

"Are we not going to wait for the King?" Holly asked.

Stella laughed. "Don't be silly. He's no King. He's an idiot," she said with a mouth full of bread. Tom threw his hands up like what!

"Why didn't you tell us this before we decided to come here?" He asked vehemently. Stella paused, staring at Tom as if he had lost his mind, then she thought about his question. She shrugged her shoulders after swallowing the last bit of bread. "Because I'm the one who can help you. Plus, that idiot made you two believe you had a choice. When in reality. If you had said no, he would have let you go. But," she said with a pause as to make her point sink in... "he would have sent his men to either bring you back or kill you."

Holly instantly asked, "Do you know why we are here?" Stella pushed her chair back from the table and stood. "No, not exactly, but I do know it has something to do with our powers."

"What powers?" Tom asked.

"Most of the people born of this world have powers. Some can make objects appear, and some can make them disappear. Some people can create tunnels, allowing travel from one world to another. It had to be one of those tunnels that you came through." Stella paused in her thoughts, and Tom looked at her and asked another question. "Do you know who created that tunnel?"

Stella reached over Holly's shoulder and picked up a piece of cheese from her plate. "I believe it could have been the old man you are searching for. He came here a few days ago. I overheard him and Dusten, the King as you know him, talking about two people coming from another world. I don't know which, but it seems one of you has powers he and

Dusten need. I don't know for sure, but I believe we can trust the old man."

Realizing she should have followed the letter, Holly asked Stella, "Do you know where we can find him?" Stella nodded. "Yes, I talked to him while he was here and learned things aren't as they seemed for me. I don't know what the old man meant by that, but he said if I helped the two of you, he would reveal what he knows about me. As a matter of fact, I was on my way to find you when I got lost on the mountain. Dusten was also looking for you when he found me."

"Is there any way we can escape from here?" Tom asked.

"Yes, but we must wait until we enter the Castle."

"What do you mean to enter the castle? Where are we now?" Holly asked.

But before Stella could answer, the King entered the room. He had changed his clothes; he wore a black outfit similar to the one the carriage driver had worn instead of the red robe. "Are you enjoying your food?" he asked.

"Yes, we are, and thank you, but now we want to know why we are here," Holly said.

"In time, young lady, I assure you I will explain everything. For now, since we have all had a long journey, we must rest. Stella will show you to your rooms. I will see the two of you in the morning."

Without another word, the King left the room. Tom stood up and walked toward the door where the King had exited. Stella stopped him in his tracks. "Not that door! We must go back through the door we came in." Stella yelled. "Come, I'll show you." Taking Holly's hand, she led her toward the door. Holly followed Stella through, But Tom hesitated a few seconds before following them.

The bright light hit him, spinning his body in mid-air. The light changed from white to blue to green and then back to white.

4

The King's Control

Holly and Stella came out of the tunnel at the same time, standing inside a grand ballroom. Music was playing, people were dancing, and others were standing around talking in small groups. Holly's eyes searched the room and then grabbed Stella's arm. "Where is Tom?"

Stella looked around and pointed toward the stairs. "Let's ask him," she said. As the King exited the stairs, Holly ran to meet him. "Where is Tom?" she asked. The King smiled. "Calmed young lady. I have sent him on a small mission. He will be joining us shortly." he said.

Stella watched as the King led Holly to his table. When the King stopped to talk to some of the people, she walked over and sat beside Holly. "I have a friend who lives a couple of miles from here. He will help us find the old man. But we must leave tonight," she said. Holly shook her head from side to side. "I'm not going anywhere without Tom."

"We will talk about this later," Stella said as the King approached the table. Holly wanted nothing more than to leave the Castle, but not without Tom. As if reading her mind, the King touched her hand. "It may take time, but you will learn to like it here," he said.

The night seemed to drag by as Holly kept her eyes glued to the door she and Stella had emerged from. Seeing Holly's discomfort, Stella stood up, pushing her chair back from the table. "It's getting late. We need to get some sleep," she said. Relieved at the suggestion, Holly followed Stella up the stairs, down a long hallway, and into an empty room. Stella raised her hand, and one of the walls disappeared, revealing another room. "Follow me."

Once inside the room, Holly turned around in time to watch the wall reappear.

"How did you...?"

"It's one of my powers," Stella said before Holly could finish her question. A long rack of clothes hung along one wall. Stella picked out two black outfits and handed one to Holly. "Put this on. We need to leave as soon as possible."

"No! Stella. I have already told you I'm not leaving this castle without Tom." Stella reached out and grabbed both of Holly's arms. "Listen to me, Holly. Tom is still inside the tunnel. Dusten will hold him there until you do whatever he wants you to do. If you are not here, he will release Tom and try to use him to find you. I have already told you I have a friend who can help us find the old man. I believe he will also be able to help find Tom. My friend has special powers. He can at least tell us where Tom is."

"How do I know I can trust you?" Holly asked.

"You don't, but you will have to trust someone sooner or later, so it might as well be me," Stella stated.

Holly nodded her head in hopes Stella was telling the truth. She quickly changed her clothes and asked, "How do we get out of here?"

"Stand back. I'll show you." Holly backed up against the wall, watching Stella walk in a complete circle. When Stella stomped her foot, the floor opened, revealing a passageway into a cave. Holly followed Stella inside. The floor closed, leaving them in the dark. Holly couldn't see her hand in front of her face.

"Stella, where are you?" she yelled. At that moment, a bright light appeared in her left hand. Holly screamed, shaking her hand. Stella wrapped both arms around Holly, holding her tight. "Calm down; it appears you also have powers in this world."

"Please, Stella, let me go. I'm kinda freaked out here. Where does this light come from?"

"I'm not sure. Are you afraid of the dark.?" Stella asked as she let go of Holly and stepped back. Holly moved her hand, shining the light from side to side before she answered Stella.

"Yes, and are you telling me our powers are created from our fears?" Holly asked.

"For some people, it takes some drama to reveal their powers. In time, they learn to use them at will." Stella stated.

One hour later, Holly followed Stella out of the cave. When the cave closed, Holly took in her surroundings.

They were standing inside a barn with bales of hay lined against one of the walls. There were three stalls, with two horses each, and a young man stood beside one of the stalls.

"Holly, this is Neal, the friend I told you about."

"Nice to meet you," Holly said.

"It's my pleasure. I have prepared a room for the two of you."

Holly looked at Stella and then back at Neal. "How did you know we were coming?" she asked. Neal chuckled before answering, "I have what my mother calls a gift, although sometimes I see it as a curse. I can see things before they happen. Sometimes good, sometimes bad."

Holly nodded; with all that had occurred, she took the explanation without question. "Stella said you could help me find my friend Tom." Neal looked at Holly and gave her the best possible answer. "Yes, maybe, but it's late. We must sleep. We will talk more in the morning," Neal said.

Holly followed Stella and Neal out of the barn. The house looked like any other house in her world. Once inside, she could tell Neal lived alone. The house was clean, but in her opinion, it needed a woman's touch. There were only two bedrooms, so she and Stella shared a bed. Stella went straight to sleep while Holly lay awake, thinking of Tom and hoping he was safe.

The next morning, while eating breakfast, Neal looked at Holly. "Your friend will enter the castle tonight. He will escape and journey here. Then...," Neal looked at Stella. "Then what?" Holly asked. Neal shook his head. "Then we will need to leave this place. The king and his men will come. They will burn my house and barn." he said.

"Is there any way we can stop them?" Stella asked. Neal looked at Holly. "There is always a way to change the future. Isn't that why you are here?" he asked. The question took Holly by surprise. "Look, Neal, I don't even know where here is, much less why I am here. For all I know, this entire situation could be some kind of sick dream."

Neal slammed his hand down on the table, causing Holly to jump back from him. "I'm telling you, this is not a sick dream. Ever since you people started coming into this world, bad things have happened. That idiot who calls himself a king has killed hundreds of people, including my mother and father!" he yelled. Tears ran down Holly's face. "I'm sorry, I really am, but I still don't understand what this has to do with me."

Stella walked over and put her hands on Neal's shoulders. "Please, Neal, calm down. You yourself said there is always a way to change the future. I know we will be able to figure out a way to save this farm," Stella stated.

Neal walked into his bedroom, closing the door behind him. A few minutes later, he returned. He kneeled beside Holly, placing his hand on her arm.

"I'm sorry I yelled at you. I don't know why you are here. I do believe the old man will be able to help you figure that out. Tomorrow, we will meet your friend at the bridge that crosses the grave ditch."

He looked at her as if she knew the location he was talking about. Holly shrugged her shoulders. "It's not far. It's where the king's men buried all the bodies of the people they killed," Neal stated, finalizing his thoughts.

"Why did the king have all those people killed?" Holly

asked. "As you should already know, some people in this world have powers. All of our powers come from a source. He doesn't know where the source is located, but he believes someone knows. He had the people brought before him, and when they said they didn't know where the source was located, he had them killed. When this didn't pan out for him, he tried another tactic. He sent some of our people to another world in search of the source."

"Do you know where the source is?" Holly asked. Neal looked at Stella, who nodded her head. With permission, Neal continued talking. "Yes, our powers are given to us by the Queen, Stella's mother."

"Where is Stella's mother?" Holly asked curiously.

"We don't know. The Queen has been gone a long time. I do believe the old man knows where she is."

Holly looked at Neal and was about to ask another question, but Neal held up his hands to stop her. "Okay, no more questions. Right now, we need to put our heads together and figure out a way to meet your friend and make our way to the mountain before the king and his men come here."

Stella sat down next to Holly. "I have an idea. Do you have trucks in your world?" she asked. "Yes, why do you ask? Holly said. "Not long ago, a man came to the castle. He was able to transport objects from one world to another. He brought this green box thing. It moves across the ground by itself. He called it a truck. I have ridden inside it twice. I believe I know how to make it move." Holly smiled. "Yes, we do have trucks.

I haven't driven much, but I know how to make it move. Where is this truck?" she asked. "The man who brought it here died. The king's men pushed it behind the castle."

Neal closed his eyes. A few minutes later, he stood, kissed Stella on the top of her head, and smiled.

"This will work. Different events change events, which changes our future. Holly will drive the truck to the bridge, where we will meet your friend and then make our way to the mountain. We will leave the truck at the base of the mountain and continue on foot. In my vision, I saw us on the mountain. We were safe. I couldn't see beyond that point, but once we get there, I will be able to see more."

"The truck has a guard sitting inside it at all times. How will we get it?" Stella asked. Neal walked over to a cabinet, opened a drawer, and brought out a small handgun. He lay it on the table in front of Holly.

"This is a .22 revolver," he said.

Holly looked at the gun and commented on Neal's thoughts. "I know what it is. My father has lots of guns, but what are you going to do with that?"

"I will place the gun in a basket. Stella will use her powers to create a cave. It will open behind the castle. You will carry the basket, and as you approach the truck, the guard will think you are bringing food. He will step out of the truck, and then you will remove the gun from the basket and shoot him. At that time Stella and I will join you. You will make the truck move to the bridge. From there, your friend will take us to the mountain."

Holly shook her head. "No… I can't kill anyone."

Neal smiled. "Yes, you can. I saw it in my vision."

~~~~

Tom stood inside a grand ballroom when he opened his eyes. A band played music. At least one hundred people
~~~~

mingled around talking. He walked around the room looking for Holly. A young woman bumped into him.

"Excuse me, I'm sorry," she said. Tom reached out and grabbed her arm. "Hey, I'm looking for my friend—a young blonde woman. She came in here with Stella." At the mention of Stella's name, the music stopped. The room got quiet. A large wooden door opened. Two guards came in, pointing their rifles at him.

"What color was the light?" one of the guards asked.

"What light?" Tom asked.

"The light in the tunnel, what color was it?"

Tom had to think. "White, blue, green, hell, I don't know," he said. The two guards turned and left the room, closing the door behind them. Tom realized he was still holding on to the woman's arm. He let her go, stepped back, and asked, "What was that all about?" The woman smiled.

"I think you were inside the tunnel for two days. I say this because the woman you are looking for came through here two days ago with Stella."

Tom shook his head in disbelief. "That can't be; we were all together a few minutes ago."

The woman helped him with a bit of understanding, "Time does not exist inside the tunnels." Tom nodded before asking, "Do you know where I can find Stella and my friend?"

The young woman stepped back as if wanting to end the conversation. She looked around the room before she spoke. "No, they left the castle. The king and his men are searching for them." The young woman turned and walked away.

"Wait. One more question. Where does that door lead to?" Tom asked.

The young woman looked over her shoulder and quietly stated. "We are on the roof of the castle."

Tom walked over, pulling the door open wide enough for him to slip through. He came face to face with one of the guards. He didn't take the time to think about what he needed to do. He kicked out with his right foot, striking the guard in his groin. When the guard fell, Tom reached down and snatched the rifle from the guard's hands. Two more guards ran toward him. He pointed the rifle in their direction and pulled the trigger. The rifle jerked twice in his hands. Both guards went down. There was a four-foot rock wall around the roof. Tom saw a rope ladder coiled on the floor with one end attached to the top of the wall. He picked it up and tossed it over. A bullet hit the wall inches from his head. Chips of rock stung his face. Three more guards ran towards him. He pointed the rifle in their direction, pulling the trigger until the rifle stopped jerking. He dropped it on the floor and dove over the wall.

He fell twenty feet before he was able to grab the ladder. The force of his weight slammed him against the wall. Letting his feet hang free, he worked his way down the ladder using his hands. A few feet from the ground, he let go. Within seconds, he was up and running. He had only taken a few steps when he realized he was falling. The cold water took his breath. He fought to the surface and swam across the moat as fast as he possibly could.

After clearing the moat, he ran across an open field. He could see the outline of the trees ahead of him, and he heard the bullets hitting the ground behind him. He mustered all of his strength and ran faster. Tom was well inside the trees before he stopped running. He held onto one of the trees while trying to catch his breath. Tom could see the light from the torches atop the castle wall. Figuring he was safe and hoping the king's men wouldn't come hunting him in the dark, he lay beside a fallen tree. His mind raced. At one point, he slapped himself, hoping it would wake him from the nightmare he found himself in. He drifted in and out of sleep until morning.

Waking from his sleep and wondering about the king and his men, he moved cautiously from tree to tree until he could see the castle. The drawbridge had been lowered. Men on horseback lined the field beyond the moat. The king stood atop his carriage. Tom couldn't hear the king's words but knew he was giving the men instructions. Tom watched as two of the men rode toward the mountain. The remaining men followed the king's carriage around the castle. Tom remembered seeing several farmhouses along the road when he rode in that carriage. He knew farms meant barns, and barns meant horses.

Tom began moving from tree to tree until he stood at the forest's edge, studying the terrain. He would need to run half a mile to the bridge, then another hundred yards to the farmhouse. He couldn't think of a reason to delay any longer. He needed a horse to return to the mountain to find the old man. But more importantly, Tom knew he needed the old man to help him find Holly.

5

The Old Man

Holly followed Stella and Neal back inside the barn. Stella walked in a circle and stomped her foot. When the ground opened, she looked at Holly. "You will need to do your thing with the light." Holly looked at both of her hands, trying to will the light. When nothing happened, she looked at Stella, confused.

"Come, let's go inside the cave. I believe your fears will kick in once you are in the dark, and the light will appear." Stella was right. When the cave closed, Holly's hands lit up. She led them through the cave until they were near the end. "The two of you wait here. I need to see exactly where we are," Stella said. Neal and Holly stood silently watching as Stella exited the cave. A few minutes later, she returned. "How does it look?" Neal asked. "Like a piece of cake. We can hide behind a large tree when we step out," Stella said as she reached out and touched Holly's arm.

"Are you sure you can do this?" Stella asked. "At this point, I'm not sure of anything. All I know is I need to find Tom, and I'm willing to do whatever it takes," Holly replied.

"Okay, let's go," Neal said as he handed Holly the basket. She carried it in her left hand with her right hand inside the basket, holding the gun. She was looking at Tom's truck. She knew it wasn't actually Tom's truck, although it was the same make, model, and color. When the guard saw Holly, he stepped out. He lay his rifle on the back of the truck and walked toward her. Although Holly was nervous, she forced a smile. When the guard was a few feet away, she pulled the gun out of the basket and shot him. Neal and Stella walked out from behind the tree when the guard fell. Holly stared at the guard. Her whole body shook, and she kept repeating, "I can't believe I just killed someone."

"Come on, we need to hurry," Neal said, snapping Holly's mind back to their mission. She gulped as she felt her insides reach her throat. She forced herself to think about Tom and mentally convinced herself killing the guard wasn't real to justify her inner conscience. Holly moved into action after gaining some semblance of control and got behind the wheel. Neal climbed inside the truck, and Stella slid in beside Neal. Holly pushed in the clutch and turned the key. The engine turned over a few times, then roared to life. Holly pulled the gear lever down in first, turned the truck around, and drove straight for the bridge.

Tom was halfway across the bridge when he heard the truck horn blowing. He couldn't believe what he was hearing and seeing. His own 1972 Ford truck was coming straight towards him. At that moment, he believed the king's men had caught him. Knowing he couldn't outrun the truck, he stopped and raised his hands above his head. The truck slid to a stop beside him. Again, he couldn't believe what he saw. Holly climbed out of the truck. She threw her arms around him. "I thought you were lost," she said.

After a few moments, Neal tapped Holly on her shoulder. "I hate to break up this little reunion, but we must go now," he said. Holly slid across the seat. Tom got behind the wheel as Neal and Stella climbed onto the back of the truck. Tom pushed the gas pedal to the floor, then asked, "Where are we going?" Looking ahead, Tom saw two men riding towards them on horseback. He heard two gunshots, and both men fell to the ground. Tom stopped the truck beside the two dead men. Neal jumped off the back of the truck, holding a rifle.

"Where did you get that?" Tom asked. "It was in the back of the truck. It must have belonged to that guard Holly killed," Neal said. Tom looked at Holly. She shrugged her shoulders with a little shudder. "We needed that truck," she said, more confident than she felt.

"Here they come!" Stella yelled. "Get those guns from the dead men. We will be able to outrun the others," Tom said. Within seconds, the four of them were back inside the truck, leaving the King and his men far behind.

Tom parked the truck at the base of the mountain. Although they were miles away, the king and his men were still in sight. Neal walked over to Tom and stuck out his hand. "Hi, I'm Neal."

"Yes, Holly told me everything. Thank you for helping us." Tom said as he shook Neal's hand. "What do we do now?" Holly asked. "We could stay and fight," Stella said. "No, we only have three rifles and at least thirty of them. We must go up the mountain," Neal said.

Stella took a few steps up the path, then turned back to face the others. "There are two paths over this mountain. One will take a lot longer than the other. We must take the longest route. I know the king. He and his men will take the shortest. He will believe we are ahead of them when they reach the river. When he finds out we aren't, he and his men will turn back. By the time we reach the river, they should be gone."

"Why can't we use the road we traveled while in the carriage?" Tom asked. "That road doesn't exist. One of the men who drives the carriage also has powers. He created that road and made it vanish once we were off the mountain." Stella said. "What stops him from creating another road instead of taking the path you told us about?" Holly asked.

"He won't be with them on this trip," Stella said.

"How do you know that?" Holly asked.

"His name is Markee, and he is my friend. While you and Neal slept, I returned to the castle and talked to him. He promised he wouldn't help the king search for me anymore. I still believe the longest path will be our best bet."

"Wait a minute," Tom said. "Let's think this through. What if they split into two groups, and some of the men follow us?" Stella pointed up the mountain. "About a mile up, we will come to some flatland. We will be able to watch our backs from there." "All of you listen to me, Neal said. "None of you have to worry about the King and his men. We will make it to the river. I have seen it in my vision."

"How could he know that?" Tom asked. "He has powers

that allow him to see the future," Holly said. "Then he should be able to tell us when we can go home," Tom said.

Neal walked up next to Tom. "My powers don't work like that. I wish they did, but the reality is sometimes I can see two or maybe three days ahead. Most of the time, I can see only a few hours ahead."

~~~~

Three days later, the four of them sat beside the river. Neal sat on a fallen tree and closed his eyes. When he opened them, tears ran down his face. "I can't go with you," he said. Tom realized Neal was talking to Stella. "Why can't you go?" she asked.

"In my vision, I see the four of us shooting it out with some of the king's men. Next, I see the three of you talking to the old man."

Holly walked over and stood beside Neal. "What does this mean?" she asked.

Stella put her hand on Holly's shoulder. "It means Neal will be killed in the fight," she said.

"No, no, no...We can change this. You said different events change things, and we did stop them from burning your farm," Holly said.

Tom walked over to the river and squatted to splash water on his face. He noticed the speed of the river's current. "The river!" he yelled.

"What are you talking about?" Holly asked.

Tom pointed at Neal. "That tree you sat on. It's been dead for a while. It should float. We can use it to go down the river," he said. Working together, they dragged the dead tree to the river's edge and pushed it into the water. Stella then
~~~~

Holly straddled the tree. Neal handed each of them one of the rifles. He removed the clip from the third before throwing it into the river. Tom held onto one side while Neal held onto the other. They braced their feet on the muddy bottom, shoving the tree into the current.

As they floated down the river, no one spoke in fear of the king's men hearing them. The water pushed them faster. Both Tom and Neal heard the noise at the same time. They reached up, pulling Holly and Stella into the water. Seconds later, the current washed them over a waterfall. They dropped twenty feet into the white water. The current swept them further down the river, sending them over a second waterfall. Tom managed to get his head above the surface. He saw Holly and Neal ahead of him. Stella was floating face down beside him. He grabbed her shirt. Fighting the current, he managed to pull her to the shore. Holly came out of the water seconds later. She placed her mouth over Stella's and blew air into her lungs while Tom pumped her chest, causing Stella to cough up a mouth full of water.

Stella opened her eyes. "What a trip," she said. Holly, Tom, and Neal looked down on her and laughed. Neal helped Stella to her feet.

"I should have seen that coming," Neal said.

"That's okay; you can't see everything," Stella said.

Wanting to stay close to the river, they walked along its shore. When he heard voices ahead of them, Neal held up his hand. "We need to get out of here now," he said.

"Wait!" Stella yelled. She ran in a circle and stomped her feet. The ground opened, revealing a cave. Once inside, the ground closed behind them. The darkness sent chills down

Holly's spine. She shook her hands, causing the lights to appear. "What the hell," Tom said. "Oh, I forgot to tell you Stella and Neal ain't the only ones with powers in our group," Holly stated.

"This can't be real," Tom said, shaking his head. Holly stepped back, shining the light on Stella's face. "Tell us, Stella, why all this drama?"

"What are you talking about?" Stella asked.

"Why haven't you used your powers before now? I believe if you had, we would have been at the old man's cabin days ago. So tell me, Stella, who's side are you on?" Stella held up her head, shielding the light from her eyes.

"I promise you, Holly, it's not what you think. I want to find this old man as bad as you and Tom. Remember me telling you I got lost while trying to find you and Tom? You see, I can create one of these caves at any time, but what I can't always do is predict where they will come out, expectantly, on this mountain. Sometimes, my barring is way off. On the day we met, I came out in the middle of a field. Several large bubbles were floating above the ground. All the bubbles had people inside them. I could hear them begging for my help. I didn't know where I was or how those people got inside those bubbles. What I do know is I never want to go back to that field, and every time I open one of these caves, there's always that possibility."

Holly saw the tears on Stella's face. She reached out and hugged her. "I'm sorry; I didn't mean to hurt you. I just want to go home," she said, then led the way through the cave.

Several hours later, with no sign of the cave's end. "We

need to rest," Neal said. Holly shook her head. "No, let's keep going. We have got to be getting close."

"Neal is right," Tom said. "What if we run into the king and his men at the end of the cave? We lost the rifles in the river, so we may need to run. We will need our strength."

Holly reached inside her coat and brought out the revolver. "We still have this," she said.

"Where did you get that?" Tom asked.

"It's the gun I used to get the truck."

Neal took the gun from Holly. He checked the cylinder. "Four bullets left," he said.

"Let me see that," Tom said. Neal handed the gun to Tom. He opened the cylinder and removed all the remaining bullets. I can tell they have been wet, but they look dry now. We still don't know if they will fire," he said.

Tom reloaded the gun and put it in his pocket. Holly, Neal, and Stella stood staring at him. "Hey, I may not be Billy the Kid, but I can shoot," he said. Who is Billy the Kid?" Neal asked. Tom laughed. "Never mind, let's get some sleep," he said.

Tom was the first to awake. The cave was dark. He reached over and woke Holly. "We need your light," he said. She led the way. A short time later, a light appeared. "It's the end of the cave," she yelled. The four of them walked out of the cave together. Stella spun around. "Something's wrong; the cave should have closed by now." She said. Seconds later, they were surrounded by the king's men. Tom reached for the gun. Holly placed her hand on his arm. "Not yet. There are too many of them." Tom knew Stella was right. Even if he took down four, the rest would kill them.

A high-pitched sound came from behind them. The king's men turned in all directions. Tom, Holly, Neal, and Stella all fell to the ground. When the sound went away, the king's men were gone.

"Where did they go?" Holly asked.

"It's the old man. He sent them away, so we should be close," Stella said.

It was one mile further down the river when they found the cabin. Tom opened the door. Holly, Stella, and Neal followed him inside. There was only one room with a fireplace, a table, and four chairs. The old man wasn't there. Exhausted from their journey, the four of them sat at the table. The room went dark. When the light reappeared, they each had a hot cup of tea sitting in front of them. They drank the tea in silence. A few minutes later, the door opened. The old man walked in. He wasn't what Tom nor Holly expected. He didn't have long white hair or a long white beard. The old man didn't wear a long white robe or a pointed hat. He was a man around sixty years of age, with short grayish hair and stubble on his face as if he hadn't shaved in a few days.

He wore blue jeans, a plaid shirt with suspenders, and a pair of black army boots. He carried a large goose with an arrow from his crossbow still protruding from its sides. He lay the goose on the floor, hung his crossbow above the fireplace, removed his hat, and hung it on a peg next to the door. He waved his hand in the air. Once again, the darkness came, and when the light returned, the room had changed. The room was larger, and there was a small kitchen, a couch, a chair, and tables with lamps facing the fireplace. Two doors indicated more rooms had been added to the cabin.

The old man walked towards the table, and with a wave of his hand in the air, a fifth chair appeared. Once seated, he looked at Holly. "You look a lot like your mother," he said. "You know my mother?" The old man gave Holly a wink. "Yes, yes, I do, and as a matter of fact, she once sat in that exact chair you are sitting in."

"Why was my mother here?"

"That's not important at this time. The important thing is you are here."

Holly pointed at Tom. "Please tell us why are we here?"

"Not so much he, but you," he told Holly.

"Then tell me why am I here?" Tom asked.

"You are here because she is here," the old man said with a smile.

Holly stood, slamming both hands down on the table, looking the old man in the eyes. "Now look here, mister. You are not making a bit of sense. Tell me now, no, tell us now why the hell are we here?" she shouted.

"Okay, okay, have a seat, young lady. You are here because I need you to do something for me, and I promise I will send you home once you have completed the task."

"What about me?" Stella asked. "Yes, Stella, you have done well in what I asked you to do, but now is not the time for your question." The older man reached inside his shirt pocket and brought out an old photograph of a man and a woman. He slid it across the table. This is a photograph of my wife and myself. It was taken a long time ago. She went out searching for berries. She wanted to bake me a pie for my birthday. I haven't seen her since that day. I was told by Dusten, or the king as he calls himself, that my wife died. He said she fell into the river and drowned. I searched downriver for days and never found her. I believe she still lives in another world." The old man reached across the table, touching Holly's hand.

"It's you who has the power to retrieve this book."

"And what power would that be?" Holly asked.

"The book is held inside a dark room. Two guards are posted inside the room at all times. You, Holly, have the power of light. I will create a tunnel to carry you inside that room. Your light will blind the guards long enough for you to grab the book and step back inside the tunnel."

"I don't know if I can do what you ask of me, but I'm willing to try," Holly said.

Tom stood up, walked over, and placed his hands on Holly's shoulders. I know you can do this. It's nothing compared to what you had to do to get the truck. Besides, I will go with you," he said.

"No, no, you can't go with her. You will be needed here," Neal said.

"Wait a minute," Tom said. "You know how this will turn out, don't you?" Neal stood up, looking at the floor between his feet. Tom grabbed him by the front of his shirt, shoving Neal against the wall. "You know what is going to happen? Why is it so important I stay here?" he yelled.

The old man put himself between Tom and Neal. "Tom, you need to listen to me. You and Holly were sent here for a reason. If you want to return to your world, you must stand down!" He yelled.

6

Price Of The Deal

Holly sat in the chair, rocking back and forth with her hands covering her face. Stella slid her chair over next to Holly. She put her arms around her. "Look, Holly, you can do this. We have already been through a lot in the past few days. Let's see this thing through." Not hearing all that Stella had said to encourage her, Holly felt a surge of emotion as she stood up, shook her hands, and willed the light to appear. "Okay, enough of this bickering. I want to go home... I'm ready. Let's do this," she said abruptly.

Sensing Holly's mindset change, the old man immediately waved his arm, and Holly felt herself floating. She found herself inside a whirlwind, and the tunnel spun around her. Holly soon felt her feet touch a solid surface, a floor, as she stepped out of the tunnel into the room. Once her eyes got accustomed to the dim light, she saw the book the old man spoke of on a table before her. Holly carefully picked up the book and then stepped back inside the tunnel. She felt herself floating again as she heard men shouting, then a loud pop. She couldn't see anyone but knew she wasn't alone. When Holly returned to the cabin, emerging from the Tunnel holding the book, one of the king's guards stood behind her. Tom pulled the revolver from his pocket and fired twice.

The room went dark, but when the light reappeared, the old man and the guard were gone. Holly lay on the floor, and blood poured from a golf ball-sized hole in her side. Tom screamed her name. He felt like someone or something had taken over his mind and body. He picked up Holly. She seemed as light as a feather when he instinctively raised her above his head and turned in a circle. He gently laid her on the floor when a surge of energy left his body. Holly slowly opened her eyes, and in a soft voice, she said, "I got it." Tom reached down, holding her tight against his body. "You sure did," he said.

The room went dark. When the light reappeared, the old man stood by the door. "How is she?" he asked. "She will be alright. Where the hell did you go?" Tom asked. "I carried the guard back to where he came from and made sure the others couldn't follow." Neal walked up to Tom and stuck out his hand. "When you stated, I knew how this would turn out, you were right. I knew Holly would get shot. I also knew it was you who had the powers to heal her. I thought you wouldn't have let her go if I told you," he said. Tom shook Neal's hand. "It's okay. I'm sorry I got angry, and you were right; I wouldn't have let her go."

The old man pointed toward one of the doors. "Through that door, I have prepared each of you a room. You may shower and change your clothes. When you finish, there will be food here on the table. I must go for now. When I return, I will send the two of you home." Stella stood up. "Wait, what about me? You told me things for me weren't as they seemed, and if I helped to bring Holly and Tom here, you would reveal what you know."

The old man sighed as he looked at her, and with a stretched-out arm, he pointed. "Go through the door, then you will know." The room went dark. When the light returned, the old man was gone. Holly opened the door. True to his word, there were four rooms. Above each door, a name had been engraved on a gold plaque. The first room belonged to Holly, the second to Tom, and the third to Neal. On the plaque above the fourth door, the name Kayla had been engraved. She dropped to her knees, covered her face with her hands, and wept. Holly rushed over to her. "Stella, what's wrong?" she asked. Kayla stood, pointing to the plaque. "My name isn't Stella. It's Kayla." She said as she opened the door, stepped into the room, and closed it behind her. Tom and Holly looked at Neal, who looked just as lost as they did. "I have no idea what she's talking about."

An hour later, Tom, Holly, and Neal showered, changed their clothes, and finished eating. Yet, the woman they knew as Stella had not returned. "I'll go check on her," Holly said. But before she had time to stand, a door opened. They stared at the opened door, wondering what was next. Then, a person emerged and glanced at Holly with a peculiar look.

The woman walked in, pulled a chair out, and sat across from Holly. She pushed the cold plate of food to the center of the table, then locked eyes with Holly. "Why are you here?" she asked.

"We were sent here ..." The woman held up her hand, stopping Holly mid-sentence. "I don't want to hear what you have already told me. I want to know who sent you and why." Holly started crying. "Honest, we have already told you everything we know," she sobbed.

"I don't believe you," the woman yelled. Tom stood up.

"Hey lady, whoever you are," stating the obvious after hearing her denounce her given name since their arrival. "Stop yelling at her. She is telling you the truth. We don't know who sent us here. I found a box next to a creek, and Holly was given a key for her birthday. When I put the key inside the front of the box's hole, we were inside what you call a tunnel. The next thing we knew, we were on the side of that mountain in front of a cave. We found a letter we believe was written by Holly's mother, Faye, telling us to find the old man. We met you and the king while on our way here, and you already know the rest, so now you tell us who you are," he said.

The woman started laughing. "Faye? Faye sent the two of you here?"

"Yes, we think so. Like Tom said, she is my mother," Holly stated.

"Well, you have not been sent here for the reason you were told."

At that moment, the cabin door opened. The old man walked in. When he saw the expression on Kayla's face, he knew he would no longer be able to hide the truth. It was the first time in his life he felt fear. He waved his hand in the air. The room went dark. When the light returned, Tom and Holly stood in a large room with bookshelves holding thousands of books lined two walls. Several beautiful paintings hung from one of the other walls, and the fourth wall had six large windows and a door. Holly walked over to a window and pulled back the drapes.

"Tom, hurry, look at this!" She yelled.

Neal and Kayla stood outside the house. Their hands were tied behind their backs. The king and his men stood behind them. Tom and Holly watched in horror as one of the king's men stepped forward, looked up at them, then shot Neal in the head. Two other men grabbed Kayla. She fought like a wild cat. At one point, she got loose from the men. She ran in a circle, then stomped her feet. The ground opened below her, allowing her to drop out of sight.

"No!" Holly yelled as several of the king's men fired their rifles into the hole before it closed. The king said something to his men. All of them looked up at the window. Tom realized what was about to take place. "Get down," he yelled as he grabbed Holly, pushing her to the floor. The room went dark. When they came to themselves, they lay on the old man's cabin floor. Tom saw the revolver lying beside the door. He picked it up and pointed it towards the old man. The old man laughed. "If you shoot me, you will never go home."

"I swear I will kill you with my bare hands," Holly said as she walked towards him. "All we have heard is lies. Lies from the king. Lies from you and Stella or Kayla, whoever she is. Right now, all we want to hear coming out of your mouth is the truth. Why was Tom and I sent here?" The old man didn't say anything. He looked toward the door. Holly slammed her hands on the table.

"Now!" she yelled. The old man pointed towards the door.

"Help her," he said. At that moment, the door opened. Kayla walked in, covered in her own blood. Tom rushed over and picked her up.

Holly took the revolver from Tom and pointed it toward the old man. "Put your hands on the table. I have already killed one man with this gun. Believe me when I tell you I won't think twice about doing it again," she said. Tom held Kayla above his head. He turned her around until he felt the energy leave his body. He lay her on the floor. She opened her eyes and smiled. "Thank you," she said as she stood and walked towards the old man. Tom stepped in between them. He grabbed Kayla by her shoulders.

"Listen to me. I don't know your plans, but whatever you do, it will not bring Neal back. We need the old man." Kayla nodded her head and then sat across from the old man. She reached out and placed her hand on top of his.

"Tell me father, why all the lies? Why have I been deceived all these years? Why is that book so important to you?" The old man looked at his daughter. "That book is the reason Holly and Tom were sent here. It has the power to release your mother." He said quietly.

Kayla shook her head. "I don't understand. Where is my mother?"

"Allow me to get the book, and I will explain everything."

"Where is the book?" Kayla asked.

The old man sighed, "I put it back inside the dark room. Not even Dusten would think to look there."

As the old man stood up. Holly raised the revolver.

"Put that thing away, you don't need it."

The old man reached inside his shirt pocket, brought out two bullets, and tossed them on the table. "Besides, I unloaded it while you were gone," he said. He raised his hand. Darkness, then light. He was gone. Tom and Holly looked at Kayla.

She pointed towards the chair. "Sit, and I will tell you what I know, but you must understand I have been tricked too. We were living in your world. I had a good life until I met Faye. You see, my mother was queen of this world many years ago. The old man was the king. Before you ask, yes, he is my father. His name is Carter Morton. He was born in your world sometime in the sixteenth century. I don't know the details. He came here as a young boy. He and my mother became friends, and once they were old enough, they got married," Kayla stated with a sigh as she looked off in thought and then back at them.

She continued, "At that time, my mother, Amber, was the only one with power. She gave my father his powers. When my sister and I were born, yes, there is a Stella. She is my twin, and we also had powers. Dusten befriended my sister. Stella was so naïve that Mother realized Dusten was using Stella's powers for his ill-gotten gain. You know, Stella has the ability to create tunnels. Dusten had her bringing men from your world and sending the yellow rock you call gold back through the tunnels. Mother gave Stella's powers a different language. She wrote them in that book. She hid the book, but Stella found it. Mother did something that caused Stella's powers to only work in the light. Even though it broke Mother's heart, she sent Stella to your world and locked her inside a dark room. This made our father angry. Then he left the castle and moved here to this cabin. During that time, Dusten declared himself king and found the book but couldn't read it. Dusten knew my mother could but didn't know where she was. He called Mother the source of our power. Many people died because they did not know where to find Mother. Some because they weren't able to read the book. He placed the book in the darkroom in hopes Stella would return. It was then that Mother gave some of our people powers. She and I moved to your world with no intentions of returning."

"Why did you come back?" Holly asked. Kayla laughed. "That, my friend, is a question you must ask Faye. I met her on our first day of college. We became friends, so I thought. She invited me to a place called Georgia. She said we were going to visit her grandfather. Without my knowledge, he opened one of the tunnels and sent me back. When I returned, I couldn't remember anything of this world, nor yours. I couldn't even remember my name. It was Dusten who found me on the mountain. He told me he was the king and that he knew me, and my name was Stella. I had no reason not to believe him. He gave me everything I asked for. He also told me about my powers, but I had to learn, or should I say figure out, how to use them."

Tom slid his chair back and stood up. "May I ask you a personal question?" Kayla nodded her head.

"You said you met Faye on your first day of college. My question is, how old are you?" Kayla laughed.

"Age doesn't matter in this world. I can remain as young as I want," she said.

Holly curiously asked, "Do you plan to return to our world, Kayla?"

Kayla's eyes brightened, "Yes, of course, I love your world, but first, I have some unfinished business here."

"Are you going to kill Dusten?" Tom asked.

Kayla turned and looked at him directly before answering. "Not right away. I plan to trick him inside one of my passageways and close it up, leaving him inside. This will give him a choice. He may die by his own hands or live in the dark forever."

Kayla sighed as she considered what she must do. Walking toward them in the small cabin, she hugged Tom and Holly. As she was about to exit, Kayla looked back over her shoulder as her hand touched the door handle. "Tell Faye I will be looking to see her," she said, and she was gone.

A few minutes later, the old man walked in. Although he knew the answer to his question, he asked it anyway. "She has gone after Dusten, hasn't she?" Tom nodded his head. He laid the book on the table. Give this to Faye. She will know what to do. He pointed toward the back door. "Go home. I will help Kayla," he said.

7

Confession

It had been eighteen days when the old man sent Tom and Holly back to their world. Faye was standing on the front porch when Walter walked up the driveway. She knew by the look on his face that Tom and Holly were back. "How are they?" she asked. "I don't know. I saw the light. I came to get you so we could talk with them together."

Tom and Holly stood in the kitchen. The gold box sat on the table. Everything was exactly as they left it. Tom took the key out of the box and handed it to Holly. He took the box upstairs and slid it under his bed. When he returned, Holly was making sandwiches. "I don't know about you, but I'm starving," she said. Both of them laughed, and Tom walked over to hug Holly. They were still laughing when a knock graced the front door. Holly jumped back, pulling the revolver from her coat pocket. Tom pointed towards the gun, motioning for her to conceal it. "We are home now, Holly."

Holly put the gun back inside her coat, then took it off and hung it on the back of a chair. "I'm sorry. It's just…."

Tom held up his hand. "I know. It's okay. It may take some time for us to readjust to what we knew as normal," he said.

Tom started for the front door. "Wait, Tom, the book?" Holly stated cautiously. Tom placed the book inside one of the cabinets. When Tom opened the door, Walter and Faye stood on his porch. Neither said a word. Holly kept glancing at her parents inquiringly as they followed Tom back to the kitchen. They all sat down at the table. Faye and Walter came in and sat across from Tom and Holly with apprehensive looks. Holly, remembering everything she'd heard in the other world, was full of questions for her mother. And she immediately voiced the most prominent question on her mind, aiming straight to the point.

"Why?"

Her parents dropped their heads before Faye looked up at her daughter guiltily. "We didn't have a choice."

Holly was about to say something but was cut off by Faye. Faye held up her hand. "I know that is not a great answer. Please allow us or me to explain." Holly nodded as Tom looked at his foster parents. He looked at them intently, first at Walter and then at Faye as she told them how she and Walter had met. Faye sighed as she started to explain their move to California and Walter taking a job that led to his injury of a gunshot wound. Walter nodded as she described how they traveled to the other world and the miracle they received with Walter being healed.

"I am so grateful for the experience because I have Walter here with me, healed, and we have lived a life many people dream about. We had you, Holly," Faye said, looking at her daughter lovingly. "And we had the pleasure of raising a young man as our own." She looked at Tom affectionately. Faye placed her hand upon Walter's, staring at him as she uttered her gratitude for their gifted blessing with the love that showed in her eyes for Walter. Faye then looked at Holly and Tom as she explained the most bizarre but life-altering concept of their living. She told them something they wouldn't have believed unless they had experienced the last eighteen days.

"Walter and I were able to return home to this world, to a different time zone, to enjoy this blessed gift." Her face shined as she looked at her daughter and Tom. The young people acknowledged the information as Faye continued to talk.

"We had to comply to receive the gift, this life we've lived. I wanted more information, but the old man said we had to send you both. He did not give us a reason but assured us of your safe return." Faye paused from talking as Holly sighed, drawing everyone's attention to her. Tom looked at her with a sideways glance. Holly had listened intently, overcoming her feelings concerning her parent's past information, her father's gun injury to healing, and then time replacement. She took all that her mother said with an understanding when it was stated. But Holly still had a lingering feeling within. She sat staring at her mother. She reached inside her coat pocket, pulled out the revolver, and placed it on the table.

"So, what you are telling me is that you don't even know what kind of world you sent us to?" Holly laughed, her tone void of humor as she continued, and Faye and Walter felt the weight of her words as she spoke. "Well, let me tell you about that world. It is evil." She eyed them both down before continuing. "Do you see that gun?" Holly pointed to it as she looked directly into each of her parents' eyes. She spoke slowly, letting each word sink in as she took time to make her thoughts known.

"I HAD TO KILL A MAN. BUT THAT IS NOT ALL, NO MOTHER, FATHER," looking at them each, "NO, THAT IS NOT ALL."

Holly closed her eyes, trying to control the emotions coursing through her. With a deadly calm expression, she looked at Tom and channeled her thoughts to her parents. "We," she pointed to both her and Tom before looking her parents dead in the eyes. "We almost drowned in a river, and Dad, you know how it feels to get shot. Well, I got shot, too, only I didn't get shot with a handgun. I got shot in the back with an M.16 assault rifle. The bullet came out of my side a hole the size of a golf ball… Yeah," Holly stated, nodding as her parents shook their heads side to side in denial of what they were hearing, not wanting to believe.

Holly continued. "If Tom hadn't been there, I'd be dead, as dead as the man who owns that gun. He got himself killed while helping us, and oh yes, Mother, we ran into a friend of yours who is now, I would say, your enemy. You do remember Kayla, don't you? Because she sure does remember you. She said to tell you she would be by to see you soon."

Walter looked at Faye upon hearing the last bit of information. "What is she talking about, Faye?"

Faye ignored everyone and the question as she stood up, walked over to the sink, filled a glass with water, and then took a sip. All eyes were on her, waiting for an answer.

Before facing the others, Faye said, "I don't know why the old man wanted the two of you sent to that other world." Tom started to say something, but Faye held up her hand. "Please let me finish, Tom." Faye walked back to the table and sat down, placing her hands on the table and then placing them in her lap as she glanced at everyone. Her eyes took on a far-away look as her mind flowed with memories. She aged for a moment as a sadness enveloped her.

Faye's voice was quiet and steady above a whisper. They sat, straining to catch her every word. Walter touched her shoulder. A slight lift of her lips formed a small smile, and Faye nodded, grateful for his reassuring gesture. Though it didn't show confidence in her demeanor, she looked at him directly, her eyes begging for understanding as she said her first statement.

"The truth is, when Walter and I went to the other world, it wasn't my first trip." Walter looked shocked at her confession but steady in his stance that she continue. Faye felt assured, and her voice became more confident. "I was only six years old, and it was me who needed healing. My mother was seven months pregnant when I was born. I was born with body defects that should have been developed by the first 12 weeks of pregnancy. I was missing half my right arm and all of my left ear. It seemed like my mother blamed me. She never took me anywhere. When I turned six, she sent me to school. All the other kids made fun of me. Most days, I didn't go to school. I would hide in the woods until school let out, then I would walk home. One day, my grandfather came to our house. He gave my mother the painting that's hanging in our barn. He and my mother yelled at one another for a long time. When my grandfather left, he carried me with him. I fell asleep in the car. When I woke up, we were in the back room at his house. The old man was there too. He told me he was taking me to a world where I would be as normal as the other children. We went inside one of the tunnels, and when we came out, we were inside the castle. There were lots of kids my age. We played ball and jump rope. I had never been so happy. I don't know how long I was in the other world, but it seemed like weeks. One day, my grandfather came out of the tunnel. It broke my heart when he told me it was time to go home. It was then he introduced me to the king. I don't know why, but I didn't like him. He gave me a picture of Stella. He told me he wanted me to find her when I got older. He told me to take her to my grandfather's house, and he would know what to do. It scared me when he said bad things would happen if I failed. Failure was not an option with the information presented to me. Nevertheless, I was sixteen when a man approached me, telling me it was time to find Stella."

Faye paused as she thought about the situation, then continued talking. "I looked everywhere. I showed the picture to everyone I came in contact with. No one had seen her. It wasn't until Walter and I started dating that I gave up the search. Walter wanted to go to school in California. I didn't. I enrolled in a college at UAB in Birmingham. On my first day there, I met Kayla. I was convinced she was the one I was looking for. I thought maybe she had changed her name. I didn't care and didn't ask. I got as close to her as she would allow. I invited her on a road trip to Georgia. I told her we were going to visit my grandfather. It wasn't until after he had sent her through the tunnel that he informed me she wasn't Stella. He said he had fixed it so the king wouldn't know the difference. I drove home that day and told Walter I would visit California with him. I don't know who sent those men to shoot Walter. I didn't want to believe it was the old man, but in the back of my mind, I always knew it could have been him. It was the old man who told Walter about my grandfather after he healed Walter. I trusted him, but now one thing is bothering me. He told me the two of you wouldn't remember any of this."

Holly looked at Tom. "Get the book," she said. Tom retrieved the book, laid it on the table, and then pushed it over in front of Faye. Faye looked at the book in shock. Unable to control her thoughts and emotions, she hung her head, covering her face with her hands. Walter, Holly, and Tom looked at her, observing her with the question of what now was etched on their expressions. When Faye finally looked up, her eyes darted from the book to each of them. She then slumped in her chair and leaned as if she was about to fall over.

Walter steadied her with his hand on her shoulder. She jumped at his touch as she glanced again at the book. Guilt washed over her. Her eyes grew big, staring at the book as if it were a plague, an omen that would reach out and take her. She shook her head from side to side as if what she was seeing was a figment of her imagination. When she was able to control her emotions, she looked at Holly. "I still haven't told you the whole truth," she said. Walter shook his head.

"You mean there's more?" he asked.

"Yes, when we sent Kayla through the tunnel, her mother tried to stop us. My grandfather turned her into a statue made of stone. He placed her inside the Tropical Gardens at the Zoo in Birmingham. I have visited her every year on your birthday. I don't know if she could hear me. I always told her how sorry I was. My grandfather told me one day that I would find the words to free her. I believe this book holds those words." Faye picked up the book and proceeded to walk out the door. "Mother, wait!" But Faye never looked back.

~~~~

Walter was asleep when Holly entered his room. He hadn't spoken to anyone since Faye left. She kissed him on top of the head. "We will find her," Holly whispered. Tom was waiting at the table when Holly walked in. The gold box sat in front of him.

"Are you sure you want to do this?" Holly asked.

"It's not a matter of want. We have to do this."

"Yes, we do," Holly said as she pushed the key into the box and turned it.

Instead of a bright light, the tunnel was dark. Tom and Holly felt their bodies being pushed forward, and they were both relieved yet fearful when the movement stopped. Tom looked around.

"We are in the castle," he said.

"Where do we go from here?" Holly asked.

Before Tom could answer, a voice came from behind them. "I thought the two of you would show back up here."

When they turned around, Kayla stood at the bottom of the stairs. "Have you seen my mother?" Holly asked. "It's
~~~~

good to see you, too," Kayla said. Holly walked over and hugged Kayla.

"I'm sorry. Really. How have you been?" "I'm okay. The answer to your question is yes. She and my mother came through the tunnel yesterday. They went to see my father, and Mother said she was going to take away his powers; then she was going to close all the tunnels leading to the other worlds."

"If she closes all the tunnels, how will we get home?" Tom asked.

Kayla laughed. "Don't worry, Tom. Mother will be able to send you home."

"What about Dusten?" Holly asked.

"I took care of him myself. Mother took care of his men. Come, I'll show you two."

Tom and Holly followed Kayla to the roof of the castle. All of Dusten's men were trapped inside a giant bubble. "Mother said she would send them away when she returns." Tom looked over the wall. He remembered the last time he stood atop the castle. Looking down at the moat, he laughed. "What's so funny?" Holly asked. " Oh, it's nothing," he said. The bubble holding the king's men disappeared. "Where did it go?" Holly asked. "To a place where they will never again be able to hurt anyone."

Holly, Tom, and Kayla turned around, facing Kayla's parents, Amber and Carter.

"Where is my mother?" Holly asked.

"I know this may be hard for you to understand, but your mother betrayed both Kayla and me," Amber stated, not looking at Carter as he sighed, which annoyed Amber. But she continued speaking.

"For this, she must be punished. I have placed her at the zoo. You may visit her there. In time, she will eventually be released to carry on with her life." Amber waved her arm in the air. The floor trembled beneath their feet, and the castle melted away.

8

Stella or Kayla

Three years later....

Tom sat on his front porch watching Holly play with little Tom, who would turn two in a few days. After their return from the other world, Holly and Tom united in marriage, and a year later, little Tom was born. Faye was grateful to have been released from the statue; after missing so many memorable moments, she didn't want to miss her grandson's birth. All of their lives seemed to have returned to normal.

The sun was falling behind the trees across the road from Tom and Holly's home when something caught Tom's eye. His first thought was *a deer,* and heading inside the house to get his rifle. Then, he inwardly laughed at himself. It was the middle of August and clearly not deer hunting season. Observing the gait of the being more closely, Tom stood when he realized it wasn't a deer.

A young woman walked out of the woods. She took a few steps onto the road and then fell. "Get the truck!" Tom yelled as he ran past Holly and little Tom, who was playing in the yard.

Sensing his urgency, Holly picked up their son and ran for the truck without questioning Tom's demand. After strapping little Tom in his seat, she sped down their driveway and onto the road, stopping the truck next to Tom and the woman. Holly jumped out and lowered the tailgate. Tom gently laid the fallen woman onto the back of the truck before climbing up beside her.

Holly drove the truck carefully back to the house, avoiding as many bumps as possible. Tom carried the woman upstairs. Holly led the way with little Tom in her arms; she entered their guest bedroom, and Tom followed, placing the woman on the bed. He stepped back, watching Holly gaze at their guest.

"Which one do you think she is?" He asked as he took little Tom from her arms and placed him on the floor to play with a toy.

"I can't tell them apart, but I believe Mother will know. She was at her office when I called. She should be here in a few minutes," Holly noted after checking the woman's pulse. For a moment, as they gathered themselves mentally, they watched little Tom in silence as he started to crawl towards the bed. Holly and Tom looked at each other. In sync, a thought passed between them. "I'm going to take him to Kim's house in Marbury," Holly stated with concern.

Tom nodded. "Yeah, that is a good idea. He doesn't need

to be in any of this, nor do I want him to. I'll stay with her and wait for your mother's arrival."

"I'll be back as soon as I can," Holly stated as she picked up little Tom, who protested about being pulled from his play. Holly kissed her son's chubby cheek, and Tom did the same on the other side, distracting the toddler. Tom touched Holly's back near her waist in a gesture of endearment and stated he'd see her later as Holly looked at him lovingly. He watched Holly as she turned and left the room. With deep concern, Tom looked up to the ceiling with a what-now expression before dropping his head and looking at the unconscious woman.

~~~~

Holly returned to see her mother's car in the driveway. When she entered the house, she felt Tom's energy all around her. She looked at the staircase and quickly went upstairs. Upon entering the guestroom, she saw Tom holding the woman above his head. Holly couldn't or didn't want to believe Tom still had his powers from the other world. Neither she nor Tom had tried to use the powers since returning home. Tom placed the woman back on the bed. As soon as he stepped away, she sat up and smiled at him.

"The two of you look older," she said.

"It's been three years," Holly said. Tom stepped closer to the woman.

"Which one are you," he asked.

"It's me, Kayla."

"How do we know for sure? You look the same as you did
~~~~

the last time we saw you," Tom said. Kayla laughed. "I assure you, it is me."

Faye walked into the room, interrupting their interrogation. "Tom, if you will excuse us, I need her to take off that shift so I can look at that wound." Still looking at Kayla curiously, he informed Faye there wouldn't be a wound, stating his powers healed her. Faye looked at him skeptically, then thought about it and accepted his explanation.

After a few moments, Holly's curious mind wanted answers. "Why are you here, and who shot you?" she asked out of concern and sternly blunt—a change of her character since returning home from the other world. Kayla began to rub her clothes, feeling unclean, and pleaded with Holly with her eyes before she spoke.

"Please, Holly, may I take a shower and change these clothes? I feel so…."

"My apologies," Holly said, cutting Kayla off after she took inventory of Kayla's appearance. Kayla put her hand up. "No apologies necessary; I'm grateful, and Holly, I promise I will explain everything as best I can."

Holly nodded. "Thanks, Kayla. I will get you some of my clothes, and we will wait for you downstairs.

~~~~

Faye and Tom went downstairs with Holly, leaving Kayla to tend to her needs and rest upstairs for a while. Faye phoned Walter, and after he heard all that had occurred, he came over immediately. The four of them sat around the kitchen table.

"What does she want?" Walter asked, concerned about her mere presence in their world. "We don't know," Holly said.
~~~~

Walter shook his head, "I tell you, I have a bad feeling about this," he stated.

"Yeah, me too. I'm going to get some air," Tom said as he thought about his family and the peacefulness of the past few years. Tom stepped out the back door, only to see Kayla come around the corner of the house. When she saw him, she stopped with a look of guilt etched across her face. "What the hell, Kayla? You are supposed to be upstairs resting," he said.

"Look, Tom, I appreciate you saving my life again, but please understand, this is my problem, and I don't want to involve you and Holly. What I know and what I have to do could endanger your whole family. I'm really sorry I came here, but I was badly hurt, and I desperately hoped that you still had your powers."

Tom reached out and touched Kayla's shoulder. "Kayla, listen to me. Holly and I know if it had not been for you, the both of us would have died before we were able to return home, so I kinda feel like we owe you. Please come back inside and tell us who shot you and why."

Holly was disturbed to discover that Kayla was not upstairs and was heading outside to tell Tom when he and Kayla walked back into the house. Tom placed a fifth chair next to the table. Holly kept looking at Kayla with concern. After everyone had been seated, Kayla cleared her throat. She reached over and took Holly's hand.

"I was going to leave because I didn't want any of you to get hurt. I thought Mother had taken away my sister's powers, but somehow Stella found a way to retain them. She had hooked up with some bad men here in your world. The yellow mineral you call gold seems to be of great value here.

Stella has one of the golden boxes, like you and Tom, that allowed her to open tunnels, not only to our world but to yours as well. They transported the gold through the tunnel, and when the men returned to this world, they'd bring something evil with them. Stella left one of the tunnels open, and I came through ahead of time. I hid behind a tree. Stella and six men came through. Each of them carried a bag of gold. After Stella closed the tunnel, two of the men killed the other four, and then one of the men killed the other one. When I tried to run, the man saw me and shot me. He thought I was dead when he threw me into the river. It was then that I felt this strong power overtake my entire body. I went stiff. I couldn't move. I floated down the river and into the mouth of a creek. When I finally made it to land, I started walking through the woods. The next thing I remember is Tom standing over me."

Holly squeezed Kayla's hand, "Now I know we have to help you. You were led here by my spirit, my energy, so to speak. If you remember, the last thing I said to you -if you need me, my spirit will guide you," Holly stated.

Walter stood up. "Listen, Kayla, you have it all wrong. It's something they already have. It's called greed. This gold is worth a lot of money in this world. And money breeds power, and power has the greatest potential to breed evil. I'm not talking about the type of powers you and your family possess. It's a power that allows people to control others. People with large amounts of money can control hundreds, even thousands of people. It's that mindset that feeds the evil you talk about."

"Will we be able to stop them?" Faye asked with worry.

"Why should we stop them?" Walter asked, indifferent to the whole ordeal.

Faye considered what Walter said before stating, "Because I think for some reason we have to."

Tom shook his head…thinking about his family. "No, I believe Walter is right. Why should we get involved if what they are doing doesn't affect us? This applies to you, too, Kayla. Why not just let them do what they do?" Tom asked.

Holly looked at Kayla. "Do you have a life?"

"Yes, thanks to Tom, I'm alive."

"No, that's not what I'm asking. We know you are alive. What I'm asking is, what do you do daily in your world?"

Kayla shrugged her shoulders. "Not much. I live in Neal's house. I take care of his horses. Some days, I ride one to the mountain and sit on the back of that truck. I think about the two of you and wonder what you are doing."

"Do you and Stella get along in your world?" Tom asked.

"Most of the time, we do have our disagreements, but I never thought she would want me dead. I was curious when I went into the tunnel. I didn't know it led to this world."

"Do you know where the opening to the tunnel is?" Walter asked.

"I know where I came out, but Stella has already closed it," Kayla said as she looked at Holly.

"I know what you are thinking, and I'm sorry, Kayla. That box is long gone. Tom and I swore we would never leave this world again," Holly said.

Then, everyone looked at Faye, who immediately started shaking her head…"No, no, no! I promised Amber I would never show anyone. What I mean is No, I can't help you. I'm not going back into that statue, not for you or anyone."

Holly stood up. "Mother, are you saying you do know a way back?" "Please, Holly, don't ask me to do this. There has to be another way," Holly said as she sat back down, thinking and genuinely understanding her mother's resistance. "Okay, let me think. What about my great-grandfather?" Holly finally asked after pondering the situation for a while.

"I haven't spoken to him in years. But I will give him a call," Faye said.

"No, Mother, I will call him. This way, you and Dad will not be involved. What I need you to do is go to Marbury and pick up little Tom. Take care of him until we can figure this out."

"Now that I can do," Faye said calmly but with internal concern for her daughter.

~~~~

Early the following day, as Holly cooked breakfast, Tom descended the stairs, heading for the front door.

"Where are you going?" she asked.

"I'm going to the creek to check my bush hooks. I'll be back before you finish cooking. Wake Kayla, we all need to talk when I get back. Tom parked his truck next to the path leading down the creek. He remembered the exact location where he had thrown the box. It had been three years. He knew the creek had risen and fallen several times due to the rains. Tom knew it was a gamble, but he placed his hope on the idea that the box would be heavy enough to have remained close by. He stripped down to his underwear before diving into the
~~~~

water. It had only been three days since it last rained, and the water was still somewhat muddy. Using his hands, he could pull himself along the rocky bottom. He had to surface for air several times with no luck in finding the box. He decided to move further downstream. There, the water level was only three feet, allowing him to walk with his head and arms above the surface. He felt his barefoot strike something hard. When he reached down to rub his throbbing toe, he felt the square box.

Several thoughts went through his mind. *What am I doing? Why should I risk the life Holly and I have? Would Kayla do the same?* Then, memories of their ordeal came to mind. Had it not been for Kayla, he and Holly would not be living their life. Tom reached down into the muddy water and picked up the box. He knew this was only half of their dilemma. He didn't know if Holly still had the key. When he returned home, Holly had finished cooking breakfast, and Kayla sat at the table, drinking a glass of milk. Tom sat the box on the table before Kayla and asked for the impossible from his wife.

"Holly, do you still have the key?"

Holly curiously looked at the box and Tom's wet appearance as she answered, "No, I threw that key in the garbage the day we returned home." Kayla stood up, smiled, and clapped her hands. "Where are my pants?" she asked.

"They are on the porch next to the washing machine," Holly said.

"I have a key," Kayla said as she ran out of the back door. A few minutes later, Kayla returned holding her pants. She unzipped a small inside pocket and brought out a gold key.

"Are you sure that key will work with this box?" Tom asked.

"No, not really, but it's worth a try," Kayla said.

"Why wouldn't it work?" Holly said.

"This particular box was created for the two of you before you were born. This is the key my father used to send the two of you home, so it may or may not work."

Kayla put the key inside the box's hole. "Wait!" Holly yelled. We need to change our clothes. The last time we used that box, we came out of the tunnel on the side of the mountain with three feet of snow. If that trunk had not been inside the cave, with blankets and firewood supplies, we would have frozen to death. That time was planned, and this time, there won't be a trunk.

9

The Reunion

Faye readied herself to go, and Walter watched her with concern. "Are you sure you want to do this?" Walter asked. Faye glanced at her husband, understanding his emotions, "No, but I don't think I have a choice. I do believe Amber will understand the importance of my visit," she stated with a small smile to ease his mind.

"Yes, I believe that too, but Tom did say as long as those men didn't bother us, we shouldn't get involved. We could trust Tom and Holly with the box. They could use it to send Kayla home, and then Holly and Tom won't have a reason to go with her," Walter explained.

Faye placed the key inside the hole in the front of the box. "Yes, we could trust them; there is no doubt about that. But you and I both know Kayla believes she needs to stop Stella from whatever she is doing, and Tom and Holly will not let her go alone." Walter became silent. He knew his wife could not let her children go alone to the other world again without her. He sighed as he watched Faye turn the key. Wishing for the best, Walter watched his wife disappear.

~~~~

This was the fourth time Faye had been inside the tunnel on her way to the other world. She shielded her eyes from the bright light as her body drifted through the air. Once her feet touched the solid ground, she removed her hand from her face. She stood in the middle of a grassy field. She could see the castle in front of her. She watched as the drawbridge lowered across the mote. Six white horses came through the gates, pulling a carriage. She didn't take a step until the carriage stopped beside her.

A touch of fear set in when the big man climbed down. Her fear subsided when she saw him smile. Neither of them spoke as Faye studied the man from head to toe. He was dark-complexioned; he wore a long black coat, a black hat, and a pair of pointed-toe cowboy boots that shined like a new penny. He had two pistols strapped to his side. "Your name is Faye," the big man said. Faye chuckled at his acknowledgment and stated wittingly, "Yes, I know my name; now tell me yours." The big man took off his hat and bowed. "My name is Markee, Markee Bennett. Ms. Amber sent me."

"How did she know I was coming?" Faye asked. Markee laughed. "That, my fair lady, is a question you must ask Ms. Amber. One hour ago, she asked me to meet you here." Markee opened the door to the carriage. "If you will, Ms. Faye," he said.

As the carriage crossed the drawbridge, Faye's mind traveled back to the first time she had entered the castle. She came
~~~~

out of the tunnel as normal as all the other children, and they all wanted to play with her. It had been almost fifty years since that day. Again, a touch of fear entered her mind. It had been two years since Amber had released her from the statue, and even though she had said all was forgiven, Amber also suggested Faye should never return to her world. It wasn't so much the words Amber used but the look on her face when she said them. Markee stopped the carriage in front of the castle doors. He climbed down and opened the door. "Ms Amber is waiting for you in the dining hall. I will see you again soon, Ms Faye," he said with a bow. Markee climbed atop the carriage and drove away. Faye walked through the double doors leading into the castle. From her childhood experience, she remembered where the dining hall was located. Walking down the long hallway, she took her time admiring the wall paintings. Before entering the dining hall, the last painting stopped Faye in her tracks. It was a painting of her as a child wearing a yellow dress. Whoever painted the picture caught her at the moment, the first time she could remember being happy. Faye entered the dining hall. Amber sat alone at a small table. She motioned for Faye to have a seat across from her. There was no hello. How are you doing? It's good to see you. Amber's first words were, "Would you care for something to eat or drink?"

Faye cleared her throat. "Yes, I'll have whatever you are having," she said. Two young girls came in. One carried a plate of food, and the other carried coffee. After the food was placed in front of them and their cups filled with coffee, the young girls left the room. Faye picked up the steaming cup and smelled it. "Smells good, uh? It came from your world."

Amber said. Faye looked at the food on her plate. "It's just bacon and eggs. It also comes from your world."

Not another word was said until they had finished eating and the young girls cleared the table. "What do you want, Faye? Please tell me this has nothing to do with my daughters." Amber said before Faye could answer her first question. "I'm afraid it does. Stella has men transporting gold through one of your tunnels. Somehow, Kayla got involved and was shot." Amber stood up. Faye held up her hand. "She is fine. Tom healed her."

Amber's worried expression changed to confusion mixed with curiosity. "Tom healed her; how?" Amber asked anxiously.

"I don't know exactly. It seems Tom and Holly had powers in this world, and when they returned home, the powers came with them."

"Damn him!" Amber shouted.

"Damn, who?" Faye asked.

"Your grandfather, W.L. Benson. He swore to me he had not given your children any powers."

"How could my grandfather give them powers?"

Amber laughed. "You are naïve Faye. Do you actually believe everything in your world is as it seems?"

"No, Amber, I don't. I know some people would believe that, but you, of all people, should know that I'm not one of them. I have traveled between your world and mine three times before this one, and I know nothing is as it seems. You still haven't answered my question. How could my grandfather have given my children powers?"

Amber held up her hand. The young girl came back

carrying the pot of coffee. She poured Faye another cup and then exited the room. "Are you sure you want to hear this?" Amber asked.

Faye took a sip of coffee and tilted her head, looking into Amber's eyes. "Yes, tell me," she said with a stern conviction.

"First, you need to know I am your aunt. W.L. Benson is my father. He was born in this world many years ago. Now let me ask you this. The first time you came through the tunnel, you were, what, five or six? Your body had not fully developed. It was because your mother, my sister, also had powers, and she used them to force you out of her body too early. My father brought you here and healed you. My question is, who did you talk to other than children while you were here?" Faye thought for a moment. "Let me see, there was the woman who gave me my bath, my grandfather, and the king."

"Do you mean Dusten?"

"Yes, but he was introduced to me as the king."

"How many other adults did you see?"

"None, but I still don't understand your point."

"My point is the only thing real when you were here is the fact that you were healed from your deformity. The rest was a ploy to find Stella. They used you, Faye."

"Okay, if what you say is true, I have two questions. Why was it important that Stella be found, and why did they wait years before they asked me to find her?"

"To you, it was years. To them, not so long."

"My father has the ability to warp time to his liking. Stella somehow has powers, even I can't explain. My father believes someday, she will create a new world. A place where all the people from every world would live, and he would be the ruler. He has convinced my husband Carter, who you know only as the old man, that he could be general of the new world's royal army, but I know my father. He will discard my husband as soon as he gets what he wants. Do you know what happened to Dusten? My father kept him on a short leash until he had no use for him, and then he allowed Kayla to trap him inside one of her caves. I've never told anyone this. I let Dusten out and sent him to another world. It's my father who is removing the gold from this world. And he is using Stella to do it. Please don't ask me why because I don't know. You see, the core of this world is made of liquid gold. It gives this world the energy needed to sustain itself. Some of the liquid rises to the surface and turns to the stone your world deems valuable. There is a volcano beyond the mountain. The people from this world are mindful of gathering stones and returning them to the core. If there isn't enough to replenish, the core will be depleted, and this world will no longer exist. Neither my father nor my husband can be reasoned with. They believe the entire core will soon turn to stone, and all life in this world will die. I don't believe them. All we need to do is return all the gold stolen from this world to the core, and our world will live forever."

Faye noticed the swelling tears in Amber's eyes. But she had to ask the question.

"Now, let me ask you something. You say they have been transporting the gold for a long time, and you have all the powers. Why haven't you stopped them?"

Amber stood, slamming her hand on the table as a wave of anguish enveloped her. "Because I'm weak, Faye! Twice, I have had the opportunity to render both of them powerless, and both times, I allowed my father to convince me he would return the gold, and both times he lied."

Faye stood, grabbing Amber's arms. "Look at me, Amber. Just because you believed your father was telling the truth doesn't make you weak, and right now, at this point, we, as in you and I, need to devise a plan to stop them and keep our children safe. The men from my world have already tried to kill Kayla, and they will not think twice about trying it again."

Amber took a deep breath. "Yes, you are right. Our children's safety should come first. We will bring them back here, and then you and I will travel to your world and find the gold. I believe I know a way to return it to this world. Then I will deal with Father and Carter; this time, I will not be weak... Markee!" Amber yelled.

10

The Return

Tom, Holly, and Kayla exited the tunnel at the same time. They stood by the river, looking at the waterfall. "I remember the last time we were here," Tom said. "Yeah, that was kinda fun," Holly said. "Maybe it was fun for you, two. I almost drowned," Kayla said. "I believe we all did," Tom said.

Holly pointed toward the mountain. "At least we don't have to come down that again." Tom looked at the mountain, "It's still a long way to the cabin, Holly."

"Why are we going to the cabin, Tom?"

Tom shrugged. "I don't know. I think we are supposed to. We came out of the tunnel right here for some reason," he said.

"Yes, I believe Tom's right," Kayla affirmed as she walked in a circle and stomped her foot. The ground opened, revealing one of her caves. "And this will be a shortcut."

Tom and Holly followed Kayla into the cave. When the

ground closed behind them, Holly waved her hands, causing her light to appear, and they stood at the entrance of two pathways. "Wow! This hasn't happened before," Kayla said.

"Which way?" Holly asked.

"I don't know. As I said, this has never happened before. When we came into the cave, the river was to our left, and we knew the cabin was downriver, so I believe we should go left," Kayla said.

Holly, trusting Kayla, led the way. One hour later, the three of them exited the cave in front of the cabin.

"I can't help but wonder where that other cave led to?" Kayla questioned.

"Does it really matter? It's obvious you made the right choice. We are at the cabin." Holly said.

"Yes, I can see that, but still, I'm going to leave the cave open in case we need to go back."

"That's all good if we need to return, but let's go inside for now," Tom said as he opened the cabin door. To their surprise, Stella sat in a chair before the fireplace with her back toward the door.

"I figured the three of you would show up here," Stella said as she stood and turned to face them. "Aha, but I did give you a choice," she said.

"The other cave, where did it lead to?" Kayla asked.

Stella laughed. "Nowhere, really. But it would have had you walking in circles."

"Why'd you do that?" Kayla asked. Again, Stella laughed. "Aah, you would have figured it out eventually. I was just giving myself time to think."

"Think about what? How you were going to kill us?" Holly asked. Stella looked at Holly incredulously, "No, I have no plans of killing either of you. I was thinking about how I could convince Kayla that I'm truly sorry for what happened to her. I never meant for her to get hurt. I really need the three of you to help me return the gold or help me with a new plan to keep everyone safe."

Kayla walked over and stood toe to toe with her sister. "Stella, you and I have seldom seen eye to eye on anything. Tell me why I should believe you now."

Stella lowered her head. "That's just it. I don't know why you would believe anything I say, but I hope you will. The truth is, I never knew how important gold is to the survival of our people until I overheard our mother and father arguing about it. At first, I still didn't care, but I hope you believe now I have had a change of heart."

"What brought that on?" Tom asked, glancing curiously at Stella.

Stella's eyes looked worried. "Several things, some of them I don't want to talk about, but the main reason is I don't want to die."

Kayla saw the worry on Stella's face, "What makes you believe you will die?" Stella voiced her thoughts about what she heard, which disturbed her.

"Faye told our mother you were shot. For reasons I don't know why, but she believes I was the one who shot you. You know yourself, it wasn't me. In truth, I've never fired a gun in my life. This may be hard for you to believe, but our father and grandfather are indeed the ones sending the gold to the other worlds. I know Father knew I wasn't the one who shot you, and when he didn't tell Mother the truth, she decided having one of her children would be better than having neither of us. She told our father the dark room didn't work for me to change. She said I was evil, and if push came to shove, she would kill me herself."

"Stella, Mother may have said those words, but I refuse to believe she would actually kill you. I believe I could talk to her, and she would tell me she didn't mean it."

Stella shook her head in denial, "Really, Kayla, you believe after all the evil I've done, Mother will believe you?"

Kayla put her hands up with a little shrug before looking at everyone as she spoke... "No, not really, but I have an idea. The four of us will return to the other world to locate the gold, and then you and I will come back and tell Mother where the gold is located. She will see you are trying to help, and she will know how to bring the gold back."

"I have a question," Tom said. "What was Stella talking about when she mentioned the gold and the core being the most important to the survival of your people?"

Kayla paused before answering, thinking about his question. "Our world needs the gold, in its liquid state, to replenish the core. There is a volcano where the liquid spills onto the surface, turning into the rock you call gold. It's my understanding that a lot of people in your world have lost their lives over the yellow rock. The less gold inside the volcano, the weaker the core becomes, and if it dries up, our world will no longer exist. Take the sun in your world, for instance. If the sun dries up, your world will die, and there is nothing your people can do to stop it. However, as long as we keep replacing the gold, our world will live forever."

"Getting the gold back to our world will only solve one of the problems," Stella said.

Kayla walked over and placed her hand on Stella's shoulder. "I see you and I think alike. We also have to stop people from other worlds from coming here."

"I could do that by setting plasma rays at the entrance of the tunnels. Killing everyone who tries," Stella said.

Kayla shook her head. "No, Stella, enough people have died over this. Besides, people have been coming from other worlds for as long as I can remember. There has to be another way. Mother will know how to stop them, but first, she must stop our father and grandfather."

Kayla waved her arms in the air, and the room went dark. When the light returned, something was off, and Kayla's arms fell to her side as she stood in a daze. Amber and Faye stood inside the cabin. Kayla returned to her senses as she realized her actions, hearing her mother speak.

"We have been listening to your conversation. It's not up to the four of you to solve this dilemma. Faye and I have a plan. Tom and Holly must go home. Kayla, you and Stella are returning to the castle."

Kayla interjected, "We believe our father and grandfather are behind all...."

Amber held up her hand before Kayla could finish her statement. "Yes, we know. I will find them and give them a choice. First, this has gone on long enough, and they must allow me to render them powerless, or I will kill them both." Stella and Kayla knew their mother meant every word.

"Mother, you know what will happen if you kill our father," Stella stated as a fact rather than a question.

Amber nodded, stating, "Yes, that is why Tom and Holly need to leave this world. I will make sure Faye returns home before anything happens."

"May we have a few minutes to say goodbye?" Holly asked.

Amber waved her arm in the air. A back door appeared. "You have a half hour, then Tom and Holly must go through that door." The room went dark. When the light reappeared, Amber and Faye were gone.

"What will happen if your mother kills your father?" Tom asked. But before Tom received an answer, the room went dark. When the light reappeared, Stella had been turned into a statue.

"Why did you do that?" Holly asked.

Kayla looked at Tom and said, "You asked a good question. If our mother kills our father, all his powers will be transferred to either Stella or myself. The two of you have no idea of Stella's history. I'm not taking any chances with her. It's time for us to say goodbye. We have been through a lot together. I will never forget you. Maybe one day in the future, I will show up at your door without a hole in my chest."

Kayla hugged Holly and Tom, and then she pointed towards the door. "Now go," she said.

~~~~

After giving Markee his instructions, Amber opened a tunnel. She reached down and took Faye's hand. "Remember, when we arrive at his house, don't think about our end game," Amber stated. "Are you saying he will be able to read our minds?" Faye asked.

"He can't read mine, but he may be able to read yours." Faye
~~~~

made a hmph sound. "Don't worry about me. I can handle my grandfather. He will never know what hit him."

Faye and Amber walked up to the entrance of W.L. Benson's home, and he answered their knock on his door. "Well, this is a surprise. I never thought I would see the two of you together," he said as he turned and walked away. Amber and Faye stepped inside, closing the door behind them. "Where did he go?" Faye asked.

"I'm in the den, come and have a seat. Would either of you like something to drink?" Amber stepped close to Faye and whispered. "Don't drink anything. I don't trust him."

"Nothing for us," Faye said as they entered the room.

"Well then, tell me, what brings the two of you to my humble abode?"

"Have you seen Stella?" Amber asked.

"You came all this way to ask me a question you already know the answer to. Of course, I've seen her. She was here this morning."

"Do you know where she went?" Faye asked.

"I sent her home. She told me what happened to Kayla. I don't expect you to believe me, but I assure you neither Stella nor I meant any harm to Kayla. She wasn't supposed to be there. The man who shot her is no longer with us."

Faye glanced around the room before making her following statement. "That is another reason we are here. All this killing has to stop."

"Oh, I never said he was dead. I turned him into a catfish and threw him in the river." W.L. rather candidly.

"I didn't know you had that power," Amber said.

W.L. laughed. "I have many powers you know nothing about," he said with a hint of annoyance.

"Tell us about them," Faye stated, not as a question but as a request to be given.

W.L. sighed, letting go of a little bit of steam. He was tired of the questions and wanted to get to *the why* of their surprise visit. "Let's stop beating around the bush, can we? Tell me the real reason the two of you are here," he said while staring at his offspring of two generations.

"We want you to return the gold you stole from our world," Amber said.

W.L. stood up, walked over to a cabinet, and poured himself a drink. He looked at the high-priced bourbon, giving it a swirl in the glass. It cost a fortune for many to purchase, as it was more than $5,000 a bottle, the amount for many as a monthly salary. He looked at his liquor case. The other bourbon bottle was more than $54k. He took a sip of the bourbon, enjoying its quality and taste. As he looked at his daughter and granddaughter, the 2 ounces in his glass were worth it for the conversation. He took another sip, nodding his head and enjoying it.

Once he was seated, he looked at Amber. "You still believe what little gold I brought here will make a difference when the end of our world comes?" Amber was annoyed as he showed his inconsideration and lack of interest in their world's demise.

"Yes! I still believe if we put back the gold, the end of our world will never come!" Amber said sternly.

W.L. looked at her above the rim of the glass as he paused

to smell the aroma, "You just don't understand, do you? The end of our world will come, gold or no gold." He raised his glass to her as if to salute her thoughts and tilted his head a gesture to say *as you wish...* "If it will ease your mind on the situation." He shook his head and chuckled. Then W.L. smiled at them both...

"I'll give you back some of the gold, crazy as it is. The fruit doesn't fall far from the tree with you and your daughter. I can see where Stella gets her stubbornness."

"Why would you say that about Stella?" Amber asked, now curious.

Again, W.L. laughed. "You don't even know your own daughter. She, too, believed our world would soon come to an end. She got angry when I told her I didn't care and she should stay here with me. You know as well as I do Stella has extraordinary powers. I didn't want her using them on me. That's why I sent her home."

"Are you saying she scared you?" Faye asked.

"The truth is yes, you should have seen her. I have never seen anyone that upset. She trashed my house. After I sent her home, I was able to put everything back in order. I had just finished when the two of you arrived."

"Where did you send her?" Amber asked.

"To the mountain. I figure by the time Stella makes her way home, she would have calmed down." Amber looked at Faye and nodded her head.

"Well, grandfather, it was good seeing you, but it's time for us to go. Don't worry about Stella. We will find her," Faye said.

As Amber milled around the room, W.L. Benson raised his glass to Faye's thoughts. Once distracted by Faye, Amber got closer to her father, looking around the room at items that had been replaced due to Stella's upset. As she approached her father, she asked several nonchalant questions about putting the house in order. Once behind him, she reached and touched his shoulder, turning him into a statue. Faye walked over and stood in front of him. She looked at him remorsefully, seeing a simmer of power behind the marble, and it disturbed her. He was powerful, but she made her thoughts known with a bit of courage.

"Grandfather, you know, I've been where you are, and I know you can hear me. Once this is over, I'll bring the book here and set you free."

Amber shook her head at Faye's love for her father. "Let's go, Faye!" Never looking back, Amber reached and took her niece's hand, leading them out of the room and away from the man she felt was one of the reasons for their pending doom.

"Where to now?" Faye asked.

"To the castle. Now it's time to deal with Carter."

Faye looked back at the statue as they turned the corner. She swore she could see her grandfather's fury simmering through. The glass still in his hand looked as if it had cracked. She shook at the idea of it all.

~~~~

Tom and Holly watched as Kayla exited the cabin. "Let's go home," Holly said. At that moment, the room went dark. When the light reappeared, the door that was supposed to lead them home no longer existed.

"Something's wrong. Hurry, let's see if we can catch up
~~~~

with Kayla," Holly said. When they exited the cabin, they both stopped in their tracks. Markee sat atop the carriage, smiling down at them. Kayla stood holding the door open.

"What's all this?" Tom asked.

"You didn't think I would give up that easy, did you? Come, we have places to go and people to see," Kayla said.

"Holly, I need you up here with me," Markee said. Holly climbed atop the carriage as Kayla and Tom seated themselves inside. Markee drove the carriage around the cabin. As they entered one of Kayla's caves, Holly shined her light in front of them. Markee drove at a slow pace through the narrow passage. He exited the carriage as Holly climbed down.

"I'll see you back at the castle," Markee said as he drove away.

"What are we doing here?" Holly asked.

"We are going to lay low here until tomorrow. I believe I know where my father will be hiding. Tomorrow, we will pay him a visit for a little chat. I have to convince him to do whatever Mother asks."

She looked at Tom and Holly cautiously, gaining their complete attention with her look. "Please be warned, you two... My Father, sad to say, is the master of lies and can make anyone believe what he tells them."

They both placed their hand up like Yeah, yeah, we know.

"I've experienced that first hand," Holly said.

"Yes, me too, but I will be the liar this time. I'm going to pretend I'm Stella," Kayla stated.

"Plus, Markee will be with us. He will use one of his powers to cloud Father's mind long enough for me to turn him into a statue. I don't know how much time we will have.

If he comes to his senses, he may be able to free himself. But my plan is to talk to him while he is trapped in statue form." Kayla said.

"What will you tell him that could possibly change his mind?" Tom asked.

"The truth," Kayla said without a further explanation. Then, she looked ahead, stating... follow me as she began to walk.

Holly knew the answer to her question before she asked it, for she had been there before.

"Where are we going?" She asked.

"To the barn. I'm tired of walking. We need to pick out some horses for our journey tomorrow. You do know how to ride?" Kayla asked.

"Yes, we've rode horses before," Tom said.

After picking out their horses, the three of them went into Neal's house. Holly looked around.

"Wow, it looks the same as the last time I was here," she said sadly.

"Yes, I sleep here sometimes, but that's all. I never touch anything else, but this time we must. We need to eat. To-morrow may turn out to be a long day." Kayla said.

Tom toured the house while Holly and Kayla busied them-selves preparing their meal. He walked back into the kitchen, holding one of Neal's rifles.

"Please, Tom, put that back where you found it. No one will be trying to kill us," Kayla said.

"Where are we going to next?" Tom asked.

"Back to the cabin. If my father knew my mother was looking for him, he would hide there. It's kind of like hiding in plain sight. I believe it's a smart move. Mother would not look there."

The following day, the three rode their horses to the mountain. Kayla dismounted, walked in a circle, and stomped her foot to open a cave. She turned, facing Tom and Holly. "This should lead us through the mountain. If I'm correct, we should come out in front of the river and follow the path leading to the cabin. When we get closer, my father will know we are coming. Please keep in mind, right now, that Kayla is a statue. I am Stella, and we are going to free Kayla." They nodded and thought of Kayla as Stella and all the emotions surrounding Stella.

Once they entered the cave, Holly turned on her light, leading the way. They rode in silence until they exited. "Remember what I told you. We are here to free Kayla!" Kayla mimicked her sister to drive her point, and Tom and Holly nodded.

Carter was standing on the cabin's porch when they arrived. He looked at Holly and Tom, wondering why they were with his daughter, whom he couldn't distinguish. She informed him that Kayla was now a statue. Carter was not happy with the information.

"Who did this to her?"

Kayla had to think of something only Stella would say. "Who do you think did it? The man on the moon?"

Cursing a little for emphasis, Kayla followed up with, "I did it, but I'm here to free her." She said. Sensing Markee close by, she knew she had the upper hand.

"Kayla had it coming. I'm tired of her interfering in our business," she said.

Carter listened, nodding but suspicious of Tom and Holly. Pointing at them, he asked his daughter, "What are these two doing with you?"

Kayla looked back at them, shrugging her shoulders, showing no significant interest in them. "The same as you and I guess. They are running from Mother. Plus, this fellow..." Kayla waved her hand as if Tom was just a nobody and not worth her time, "he wants to know if you will give them a bag of the gold and then send them home?" Tom looked at Kayla with annoyance for the act... as he knew she knew his name, but calling him fellow, he loved her mimic of Stella.

Taking the bait, Carter tilted his head to the side. "Well, now, these two seem smarter than I thought. Come on in. I have some gold here, but if you want more, we must travel to the volcano," he said.

"We don't need much," Tom said as he climbed down from his horse. Kayla looked back as she stepped up onto the porch. Holly was still on her horse. "Come on, Holly, it's okay," she said.

Once inside, seeing Holly's nervousness, Kayla knew she had to work fast. She approached her father, placing one hand on his shoulder, and waved the other in the air. The room went dark. When the light reappeared, Carter stood inside a statue.

"I'm sorry, Father. I'm Kayla, that's Stella over there. I know you are probably angry right now, but you must listen to what I'm about to tell you. Whether you believe me or not, our world is in danger of being destroyed. We need that gold to replenish the core, and you know Mother will stop at nothing to get it. What I mean by nothing is -she will kill you, Father, and not lose a minute of sleep over it. You already know her powers are greater than yours, mine, or anyone else, for that matter. Father, I know I've never said this before, but I do love you. So please, I'm begging you. Save yourself. All you have to do is tell us where the gold is hidden. Mother will be able to bring it back to this world. I know you can free yourself from the statue in time, but I need your answer now."

Kayla looked at Tom. "Tell Markee to come inside." Tom exited the cabin. A few minutes later, he returned with Markee beside him.

Markee stood next to the statue. "Look, old man, you and I have been friends for a long time, and you know I've never lied to you. Kayla is telling you the truth. I suggest you tell her the truth. She is going to release you. When she does, I am going to take your power. You know it won't be long before Amber figures out where you are, and like Kayla said, she will kill you."

Markee stood behind the statue. Kayla waved her arm in the air, and the room went dark. As soon as the light reappeared, Markee placed his hand on the small of Carter's back. Again, the room went dark. When the light reappeared, Carter looked at Kayla. "You are smart. I never thought you would be the daughter to betray me," Carter said as he looked at Stella in statue form before giving Kayla his undivided attention.

"Have a seat, father. Please, everyone else outside, I want to talk with him alone."

~~~~
~~~~

With everyone outside, Kayla went and sat across from her father. "You must know I am sorry, and this is not betrayal. I'm trying to do two things here. The most important is to save our world. I'm not saying you aren't important. To me, you are, and I'm trying to save your life, and to me, it seems like you don't even care, so tell me, Father, where have you hidden that gold? Tell me, and I will allow Markee to give you back some of your powers," she said.

Carter hung up his head, looking at the floor between his feet. " I guess I should start by saying It's me who should say I'm sorry. I know we have put you through a lot. When I say we, I'm talking about your great-grandfather. But I believe you already know he is involved in all of this. I will give you back the gold, but I'm not sure he will go along with it."

"Mother will take care of him. Now tell me, Father, where is the gold?"

Carter stood up. "It's at the bottom of the river, not far from where you were shot, but you must know this. W.L. Benson has people guarding that gold; if anyone goes near it, those people will kill to protect it."

Kayla nodded, "Those people come from that world- it will not be a problem. Markee will take care of them," Kayla said. "Are you going to leave me here like this?" Carter questioned, a little fearful.

"Yes, for awhile. Once I find Mother, I'll send Markee back to return your powers, that is, if Mother will allow it," Kayla replied. "Your mother took Faye home. It would be best if you also went there with Tom and Holly. So, none of you will be here when Stella figures out how to free herself from the statue. None of you will be safe from her wrath." Carter said as he questioned whether he saw a faint light emitting from the statue. But then, upon second glance, he dismissed it as a figment of his overzealous mind at play with all that was occurring.

"I'm not afraid of Stella," Kayla said as she exited the cabin.

Tom and Holly had mounted their horses. "Unless you want to take those horses home with you, I suggest you climb down," Kayla said. Tom looked over at Holly. "Is she kidding?" He asked.

Holly shrugged and then looked down at Kayla.

Kayla smiled at them and stated. "No, I'm not kidding. If you like, you may have all three of them. I believe you will be able to give them a good home."

"Yes, of course we can," Holly said, beaming a broad smile at the thought of having three horses. Kayla mounted her horse and then took her place beside them. Markee clapped his hands. Everything went dark. When the light reappeared, Tom, Holly, and Kayla sat on the horses in front of Tom and Holly's house. After dismounting, Tom led the three horses to his barn. Holly and Kayla entered the house. "What now?" Holly said. "Now, I'm hungry. You cook, we eat, we wait. And our mothers will return here soon," Kayla said with much hope and faith.

~~~~~

Amber and Faye stood on the porch of the cabin. "Are you sure he's here?" Faye asked.

"Yes, he's here," Amber said as she opened the door and walked inside. Carter sat at the table, looking down at the floor.
~~~~~

"Is that Kayla?" Amber asked, looking at the statue.

"No, it's Stella. Kayla is the one who put her there."

"Where is Kayla?"

"They went to the other world looking for you." Amber stopped advancing toward Carter.

"Don't bother. Markee has already taken my powers. Kayla said you had plans to kill me, so I told them where the gold was hidden. She said you would know how to transport the gold back here. I will warn you as I did Kayla, W.L. has men guarding that gold, with orders to shoot on sight."

Amber laughed. "You underestimate our powers. Markee will be able to disarm those men. I will have that gold back inside the volcano by this time tomorrow. Faye and I have already taken care of W.L. Yes, I came here to take care of you, but now I have another plan. If you want your powers returned, there is something I need you to do for me."

Carter looked up. "Yes, anything," he said.

"I'm going to send you to the castle. You must gather every man and woman willing to follow you. Find them, clothe them, and entertain them. Do whatever it takes to keep them at the castle until I return."

Carter nodded, "That I can do."

The room went dark. When the light returned, Carter was gone. Faye looked at Amber. "What are we going to do with her?" she asked, pointing at the statue. Amber smiled. "I believe she will love that zoo in your world," she said. Faye laughed. "Yeah, sure, like you and I did." The room went dark when the light reappeared, and the cabin was empty.

~~~~

Amber knocked on the door of Tom and Holly's house.
~~~~

"Come in!" she heard someone yell. When Amber walked into the kitchen, Kayla stood up from the table. "Mother, we know where the gold is hidden."

Amber smiled. "Yes, dear, your father told me everything. As we speak, Markee is bringing the gold from the bottom of the river. Your father has assembled an army of men and women to help transport the gold back to our world. I've opened a tunnel. Once the last nugget of gold has been transported, I will close the tunnel forever. And that, my dear Kayla, is why I am here. I want to give you a choice. Before you met Faye, you were happy in this world."

"No, Mother, I know where you are going with this. I don't want to go back to that time. I want to go home with you," Kayla said.

At that moment, Faye walked into the kitchen, asking Kayla to excuse them. Faye took Amber's arm, pulling her away from the others. "The first time Walter and I went through the tunnel together. Carter sent us home, eliminating seven years of our lives. I overheard you asking Kayla if she wanted you to do the same for her. I was wondering, maybe..." Faye and Amber talked in a hushed tone.

Amber understood Faye as she held up her hand and smiled. She looked over at Tom and Holly and nodded her head. The room went dark.

When the light reappeared, Tom West sat on the bank of Chestnut Creek. His cane pole stretched over the water with a writing journal at his side. The red and white bobber floated gently downstream. His mind was on his friend Holly. It's her birthday. He wanted to do something she wouldn't expect. He picked up his stringer of fish and started up the path towards his truck. Halfway there, he stopped and looked around. "I swear I've done this before," he said aloud as an idea formed in his mind.

About the Author

James F. Causey, born and raised in Alabama, is a father, an avid reader, a ghostwriter, and an author who enjoys creatively writing new adventures to entertain the mind.

The Tunnel was a short story developed into a novella and was part of the first manuscript of short stories published as *Causation First Chronicle of James*. There are more stories to come—Causation Second Chronicles of James, be on the lookout.